Text copyright © 2024 by Lindy Mattice

Published by Bushel & Peck Books, a family-run publishing house in Fresno, California, who believes in uplifting children with the highest standards of art, music, literature, and ideas. For every book we sell, we donate one to a child in need—book for book. To nominate a school or organization to receive free books, or to find inspiring books and gifts, please visit www.bushelandpeckbooks.com.

All rights reserved. No part of this publication may be reproduced without written permission from the publisher.

Public-domain art sourced from the Biodiversity Heritage Library, Rawpixel Ltd., Wikimedia Commons, and TheGraphics Fairy.com. Design elements licensed from Shutterstock.com. Animal classifications sourced from Wikipedia.com.

Publisher's note: Scientific classifications for species are complex, sometimes contested, and can evolve quickly as new fossil and genetic information becomes available. The classifications and diagrams in this book are designed to give the reader a general sense of the relationships among species and should not be considered exhaustive.

LCCN: 2024930025
ISBN: 978-1-63819-128-5

First Edition

Printed in China

1 3 5 7 9 10 8 6 4 2

MAMMALIA

ENCYCLOPEDIA OF LIFE

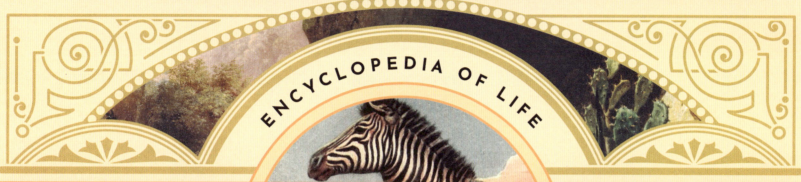

AN ILLUSTRATED GUIDE TO THE WORLD OF MAMMALS

LINDY MATTICE

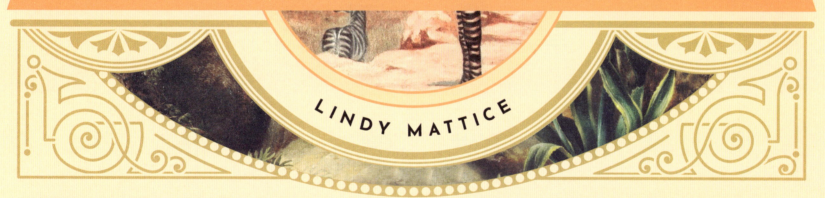

BUSHEL & PECK BOOKS

Contents

COWS, SHEEP, AND OTHER BOVIDS

Taurine Cattle *Bos taurus* 8
American Bison *Bison bison* 9
Bighorn Sheep *Ovis canadensis* 10
Astor Markhor *Capra falconeri falconeri* 11
Black Wildebeest *Connochaetes gnou* 12
Wild Water Buffalo *Bubalus arnee* 13
Alpine Ibex *Capra ibex* 14
Grant's Gazelle *Nanger granti* 15

BATS

Vampire Bat *Desmondus rotundus* 18
Egyptian Fruit Bat *Rousettus aegyptiacusfood* 19
Greater Horseshoe Bat *Rhinolophus ferrumequinum* 20
Bismarck Masked Flying Fox *Pteropus capistratus* 21

DEER

Northern Pudu *Pudu mephistophiles* 24
European Fallow Deer *Dama dama* 25
Moose *Alces alces* 26
Reindeer *Rangifer tarandus* 27

PIGS AND BOARS

Indian Boar *Sus scrofa cristatus* 30
Central European Boar *Sus scrofa scrofa* 31
Warthog *Phacochoerus* 32
Pygmy Hog *Porcula salvania* 33

HORSES, DONKEYS, AND ZEBRAS

Plains Zebra *Equus quagga* 36
Onager *Equus hemionus* 37
Horse *Equus ferus caballus* 38
Donkey *Equus africanus asinus* 40
Quagga *Equus quagga quagga* 41

RODENTS

Crested Porcupine *Hystrix cristata* 44
Domestic Guinea Pig *Cavia porcellus* 45
Northern Flying Squirrel *Glaucomys sabrinus* 46
Eastern Gray Squirrel *Sciurus carolinensis* 47
Indian Giant Squirrel *Ratufa indica* 48
American Beaver *Castor canadensis* 49
Desert Kangaroo Rat *Dipodomys deserti* 50
Northern Pocket Gopher *Thomomys talpoides* 51
Fawn Hopping Mouse *Notomys cervinus* 52
Wood Mouse *Apodemus sylvaticus* 53

MARSUPIALS

Tiger Quoll *Dasyurus maculatus* 56
Coarse-Haired Wombat *Vombatus ursinus* 57
Common Brushtail Possum *Trichosurus vulpecula* 58
Virginia Opossum *Didelphis virginiana* 59

WHALES & DOLPHINS

Blue Whale *Balaenoptera musculus* 62
Bowhead Whale *Megaptera novaeangliae* 63
Sperm Whale *Physeter macrocephalus* 64
Orca Whale *Orcinus orca* 65
Common Bottlenose Dolphin *Tursiops truncatus* 66
Harbor Porpoise *Phocoena phocoena* 67

HIPPOPOTAMUSES

Common Hippopotamus *Hippopotamus amphibius* 68
Pygmy Hippopotamus *Choeropsis liberiensis* 69

GIRAFFE

Giraffe *Giraffa camelopardalis* 71

BEARS

Polar Bear *Ursus maritimus* 74
Giant Panda *Ailuropoda melanoleuca* 75
Kodiak Bear *Ursus arctos middendorffi* 76
Grizzly Bear *Ursus arctos horribilis* 77
American Black Bear *Ursus americanus* 78
Sloth Bear *Melursus ursinus* 78
Sun Bear *Helarctos malayanus* 79
Eurasian Brown Bear *Ursus arctos arctos* 79

RABBITS, HARES, AND PIKAS

Cape Hare *Lepus capensis* 82
Woolly Hare *Lepus oiostolus* 83
Domesticated Rabbit *Oryctolagus cuniculus domesticus* 84
European Rabbit *Oryctolagus cuniculus* 85
Common Tapeti *Sylvilagus brasiliensis* 86
Arctic Hare *Lepus arcticus* 87

ANTEATERS, SLOTHS, AND ARMADILLOS

Nine-Banded Armadillo *Dasypus novemcinctus* 90

Giant Armadillo *Priodontes maximus* 91
Giant Anteater *Myrmecophaga tridactyla* 92
Southern Tamandua *Tamandua tetradactyla* 93
Linnaeus's Two-Toed Sloth *Choloepus didactylus* 94
Maned Sloth *Bradypus torquatus* 95

HEDGEHOGS, MOLES, AND SHREWS

European Hedgehog *Erinaceus europaeus* 98
Long-Eared Hedgehog *Hemiechinus auritus* 99
Star-Nosed Mole *Condylura crista* 100
Townsend's Mole *Scapanus townsendii* 101
American Water Shrew *Sorex palustris* 102
Eurasian Shrew *Sorex araneus* 103

RHINOCEROSES

Indian Rhinoceros *Rhinoceros unicornis* 104
White Rhinoceros *Ceratotherium simum* 105

BADGERS, WEASELS, AND OTTERS

Greater Hog Badger *Arctonyx collaris* 108
European Badger *Meles meles* 109
Least Weasel *Mustela nivalis* 110
North American River Otter *Lontra canadensis* 111
American Mink *Neovison vison* 112
Wolverine *Gulo gulo* 113

SKUNKS

Striped Skunk *Mephitis mephitis* 116
Eastern Spotted Skunk *Spilogale putorius* 117

RACCOONS AND OTHER PROCYONIDS

Common Raccoon *Procyon lotor* 120
Ring-Tailed Cat *Bassariscus astutus* 121
South American Coati *Nasua nasua* 122
Kinkajou *Potos flavus* 123

CATS

African Lion *Panthera leo*
Asiatic Lion *Panthera leo ssp. persica* 127
Snow Leopard *Panthera uncia* 128
African Leopard *Panthera pardus pardus* 129
Bengal Tiger *Panthera tigris tigris* 131
North American Cougar *Puma concolor couguar* 132
Jaguar *Panthera onca* 133
Bobcat *Lynx rufus* 134
Caracal *Caracal caracal* 135

WOLVES, DOGS, AND FOXES

Ethiopian Wolf *Canis simensis* 138
Plains Coyote *Canis latrans latrans* 139
Dingo *Canis lupus dingo* 140
Red Fox *Vulpes vulpes* 141
Arctic Fox *Vulpes lagopus* 142
African Wild Dog *Lycaon pictus* 143

SEALS

Bearded Seal *Erignathus barbatus* 146
Ringed Seal *Pusa hispida* 147
Harbor Seal *Phoca vitulina* 148
Harp Seal *Pagophilus groenlandicus* 149
Australian Sea Lion *Neophoca cinerea* 150
Walrus *Odobenus rosmarus* 151

SEA COWS

West Indian Manatee *Trichechus manatus* 152
Dugong *Dugong dugon* 153

ELEPHANTS

African Elephant *Loxodonta* 157
Indian Elephant *Elephas maximus indicus* 158
Asian Elephant *Elephas maximus* 159

HYENAS

Striped Hyena *Hyaena hyaena* 160
Brown Hyena *Parahyaena brunnea* 161

MONKEYS AND APES

Eastern Gorilla *Gorilla beringei* 164
Chimpanzee *Pan troglodytes* 165
Bornean Orangutan *Pongo pygmaeus* 166
Golden Snub-Nosed Monkey *Rhinopithecus roxellana* ..167
Rhesus Macaque *Macaca mulatta* 168
Yellow Baboon *Papio cynocephalus* 169

PLATYPUSES AND ECHIDNAS

Platypus *Ornithorhynchus anatinus* 170
Short-Beaked Echidna *Tachyglossus aculeatus* 171

CAMELS

Bactrian Camel *Camelus bactrianus* 174
Dromedary *Camelus dromedarius* 175

BOVIDAE

Cows, Sheep, and Other Bovids

The Bovidae family is made up of animals that are cloven-hoofed (a hoof split into two toes). They are ruminants, which means they have a four-part stomach that allows them to chew their food more than one time. Members of this family are called "bovids."

ESTIMATED NUMBER OF BOVID SPECIES 143

DID YOU KNOW? *Male bovids always have horns, but depending on the species, not every female does.*

BOVIDAE
Cloven-Hoofed, Ruminant Mammals

AEGODONTIA

ALCELAPHINAE
Hartebeest, Topi & Wildebeest

AEPYCEROTINAE
Impala

BOVINAE

BOVINI
Bison, Buffalo & Cattle

HIPPOTRAGINAE
Sable Antelopes & Oryxes

CEPHALOPHINAE
Duikers

TRAGELAPHINI
Kudus & Nyalas

CAPRINAE

REDUNCINAE
Kobs, Reedbucks & Waterbucks

OVIBOVINI
Takin & Muskox

ANTILOPINAE

ANTILOPINI
Gazelles & Springbok

CAPRINI
Chamois, Sheep, Ibexes & Goats

NEOTRAGINI
Dik-diks

TAURINE CATTLE *Bos taurus*

CONSERVATION STATUS: LEAST CONCERN

Cattle are the headline species of the family Bovidae. They're large grazing animals that have been domesticated for thousands of years. Most are kept as livestock, though some are feral (domesticated animals that return to the wild). Cattle are used as beasts of burden and raised for their hides, milk and meat, which is known as beef. Looking at a cow's face with its blank bovine stare, it's easy to think these are unintelligent animals. Yet some research suggests that cows can recognize other cows and even some people too. They can learn and remember, have emotions like fear and anxiety, and even have individual personalities.

BY THE NUMBERS	
18 FEET	*Jumping distance straight into the air*
30–40 FEET	*Jumping distance horizontally into the air*
33.5 MILES PER HOUR	*Top speed*

CLASSIFICATION

KINGDOM: ANIMALIA
PHYLUM: CHORDATA
CLASS: MAMMALIA
ORDER: ARTIODACTYLA
FAMILY: BOVIDAE
SUBFAMILY: BOVINAE
GENUS: BOS
SPECIES: B. TAURUS

AMERICAN BISON *Bison bison*

CONSERVATION STATUS: NEAR THREATENED

Bison are related to cattle and once roamed over nearly all of North America, with most dwelling in the great central plains. There is no more iconic American animal, with its great shaggy head, huge hump, scraggly beard and short curved horns. For this reason the American Bison was recently designated the American National Mammal. Though bison are commonly called "buffalo," biologists insist that true buffalo (like the water buffalo) are found only in Africa and Asia and that America's buffalo is, in fact, a bison. Bison were hunted relentlessly by white men until only a few hundred remained (the most dramatic species decline ever recorded). Fortunately, a few far-sighted conservationists helped save the bison from the brink of extinction.

BY THE NUMBERS	
400,000	Estimated population of bison today
6 FEET	Average height
2,800 POUNDS	Weight of largest (wild) bison bull ever recorded

CLASSIFICATION	
KINGDOM:	ANIMALIA
PHYLUM:	CHORDATA
CLASS:	MAMMALIA
ORDER:	ARTIODACTYLA
FAMILY:	BOVIDAE
SUBFAMILY:	BOVINAE
SUBTRIBE:	BOVINA
GENUS:	BISON
SPECIES:	B. BISON

BIGHORN SHEEP *Ovis canadensis*

CONSERVATION STATUS: LEAST CONCERN

Bighorns, as the name suggests, have really big horns that loop in spectacular spirals on either side of their head. Though females (ewes) have horns too, they're short and only slightly curved. It's the rams (males) that have the famous big horns. Rams and ewes look the same until age three. After that, rams begin growing their horns. These grow steadily during spring and summer, yet always stop in early fall during the rut, continuing to grow the following spring. This regular pattern results in noticeable growth rings, called annuli, that allow biologists to find the age of an animal. Annuli are like birthday candles—just count them up.

BY THE NUMBERS	
30 POUNDS	*Average weight of a bighorn ram's horns*
2 INCHES	*Minimum cliff-ledge width that a bighorn can stand on, thanks to their excellent balance*
300 POUNDS	*Weight of a large bighorn ram*

CLASSIFICATION

- **KINGDOM:** Animalia
- **PHYLUM:** Chordata
- **CLASS:** Mammalia
- **ORDER:** Artiodactyla
- **FAMILY:** Bovidae
- **SUBFAMILY:** Caprinae
- **TRIBE:** Caprini
- **GENUS:** Ovis
- **SPECIES:** O. canadensis

MARKHOR MARKS

Males and females share a similar tan coloring, with white underparts and a white and black pattern on their legs. Their horns flare wide at the base, just above the top of their head, with a very elongated twist.

ASTOR MARKHOR *Capra falconeri falconeri*

CONSERVATION STATUS: NEAR THREATENED

Astor markhors are a species of large wild goat that live in the high mountains of northern Pakistan and parts of Afghanistan. They are grazing animals and eat a variety of grasses, leaves, twigs, and other vegetation. Males have long hair around their chin, throat, chest, and shank area while females have short hair all over. Both males and females have a thin smooth coat in the summer months and a long coarse coat during the winter.

BY THE NUMBERS	
5 FEET	Length of males' horns
10 INCHES	Length of females' horns
8 FEET	Jumping height

CLASSIFICATION
KINGDOM: ANIMALIA
PHYLUM: CHORDATA
CLASS: MAMMALIA
ORDER: ARTIODACTYLA
FAMILY: BOVIDAE
SUBFAMILY: CAPRINAE
TRIBE: CAPRINI
GENUS: CAPRA
SPECIES: C. FALCONERI

BLACK WILDEBEEST *Connochaetes gnou*

CONSERVATION STATUS: LEAST CONCERN

Black wildebeests are commonly referred to as "gnus" due to the repeating calls the males make during mating season, which sound like "ge-nu." These common herbivores are found in southern Africa. Black wildebeests are most notable for their long white tail that looks similar to a horse's. They have a short two-toned mane that sticks out from the back of their neck and a dark brown-black coat with long tufts of dark-colored hair between their forelegs and stomach. Black wildebeests have large, strong horns that resemble hooks, as they curve forward and up. Black wildebeests are preyed on by lions, leopards, cheetahs, spotted hyenas, Cape hunting dogs, and the crocodile.

BY THE NUMBERS	
90	Percent of diet that is short grass
50 MPH	Top speed
20 YEARS	Life expectancy

CLASSIFICATION
KINGDOM: Animalia
PHYLUM: Chordata
CLASS: Mammalia
ORDER: Artiodactyla
FAMILY: Bovidae
SUBFAMILY: Alcelaphinae
GENUS: Connochaetes
SPECIES: C. gnou

WILD WATER BUFFALO *Bubalus arnee*

CONSERVATION STATUS: ENDANGERED

Wild water buffalos are large with a round chest, small, drooping ears, and horns that stretch out to the side of the head and curve upward. Females have larger horns, but the male horns are much thicker. Wild water buffalos have short, flexible legs and wide hooves to prevent them from getting stuck in deep mud and the mucky terrain of the swamps, rivers, and wet grasslands where they live (also known as riparian zones).

BY THE NUMBERS	
2,600 POUNDS	*Weight*
5–30	*Herd size*
20–30 YEARS	*Life expectancy*

CLASSIFICATION

- **KINGDOM:** Animalia
- **PHYLUM:** Chordata
- **CLASS:** Mammalia
- **ORDER:** Artiodactyla
- **FAMILY:** Bovidae
- **SUBFAMILY:** Bovinae
- **GENUS:** Bubalus
- **SPECIES:** B. arnee

ALPINE IBEX *Capra ibex*

CONSERVATION STATUS: LEAST CONCERN

Alpine ibexes are a species of wild goat that lives in the European Alps. The males have hair on their chin, as well as large horns that curve backward (the females have smaller horns). Breeding season begins in the fall when males enter "the rut." During this time, males separate from their herd and begin the search for a female herd, where a male will battle or fight against other males for mating rights. These rights allow the male to mate with every female in the herd.

BY THE NUMBERS	
10–20	Female herd size
6–8	Male herd size
10–18 YEARS	Life expectancy

CLASSIFICATION
KINGDOM: Animalia
PHYLUM: Chordata
CLASS: Mammalia
ORDER: Artiodactyla
FAMILY: Bovidae
SUBFAMILY: Caprinae
TRIBE: Caprini
GENUS: Capra
SPECIES: C. ibex

IT'S A LONG WAY DOWN

Alpine ibexes have remarkable jumping and balancing capabilities due to their sharp-edged hooves that are concave underneath. It's a good thing too—the European Alps they call home can be treacherous!

WATER TRICK

Unlike most animals, Grant's gazelles migrate into areas where water is sparse. This is beneficial because there is less competition for food from other species. They have the unique ability to live without water for long periods of time by varying their body temperature.

GRANT'S GAZELLE *Nanger granti*

CONSERVATION STATUS: LEAST CONCERN

Of all the gazelle species, Grant's gazelles have the most distinguishable white "pants" that extend up their legs, over their tail, and onto their backside. Their faces have white downward stripes, framed by black on the outside. When Grant's gazelles run away from a predator, they use a bounding leap called "pronking" or "stotting," with their backs in an arched position and landing on all four hooves. It is believed that this communicates to their predators that they are physically fit, in hopes that the predator will back down.

BY THE NUMBERS		CLASSIFICATION	
100–150 POUNDS	Weight	KINGDOM:	Animalia
		PHYLUM:	Chordata
		CLASS:	Mammalia
		ORDER:	Artiodactyla
30–40 MPH	Sustained speed	FAMILY:	Bovidae
		SUBFAMILY:	Antilopinae
		TRIBE:	Antilopini
		GENUS:	Nanger
60 MPH	Top speed	SPECIES:	N. granti

CHIROPTERA

Bats

Bats are part of their own mammalian order called Chiroptera, meaning "hand wing" in Greek. Chiropterans are the only mammals capable of flying. They use echolocation to navigate in total darkness while hunting.

ESTIMATED NUMBER OF CHIROPTERA SPECIES	1,400+
DID YOU KNOW?	Bats make up about 20% of all mammal species worldwide. They are some of the world's most important pollinators, with some plants relying on bats even more than insects to spread their pollen and seeds.

CHIROPTERA
Bats

- **MICROCHIROPTERA** — Superfamily of Microbats
- **MEGACHIROPTERA** — Superfamily of Megabats
- **MINIOPTERIDAE** — Long-Winged Bats
- **MYZOPODIDAE** — Sucker-Footed Bats
- **EMBALLONURIDAE** — Sac-Winged Bats
- **PHYLLOSTOMIDAE** — New World Leaf-Nosed Bats
- **MOLOSSIDAE** — Free-Tailed Bats
- **YANGOCHIROPTERA**
- **MORMOOPIDAE** — Mustached Bats, Ghost-Faced Bats & Naked-Backed Bats
- **RHINOLOPHOIDEA**
- **RHINOLOPHIDAE** — Horseshoe Bats
- **THYROPTERIDAE** — Disc-Winged Bats
- **MYSTACINIDAE** — New Zealand Short-Tailed Bats
- **HIPPOSIDERIDAE** — Old World Leaf-Nosed Bats
- **NATALIDAE** — Funnel-Eared Bats
- **MEGADERMATIDAE** — False Vampire Bats
- **RHINOPOMATIDAE** — Mouse-Tailed Bats
- **FURIPTERIDAE**
- **NOCTILIONIDAE** — Fisherman Bats
- **CRASEONYCTERIDAE** — Kitti's Hog-Nosed Bat
- **VESPERTILIONIDAE** — Vesper Bats

BLOOD BULLETIN

Vampire bats will chase other bats away from their food and only share with their young.

VAMPIRE BAT *Desmondus rotundus*

CONSERVATION STATUS: LEAST CONCERN

Vampire bats are the only mammal to feed entirely on blood past their first month of life. Vampire bats are small, but their size can nearly double after a large feeding. Vampire bats have extremely sharp front incisor teeth that they use to cut a 3mm incision into their prey. The bats laps up the blood from the cut using their distinct tongue, which has two lateral grooves. These grooves expand and contract, enabling the lapping movement. They feed primarily on sleeping livestock and can transmit diseases such as rabies.

BY THE NUMBERS		CLASSIFICATION
7 INCHES	*Wingspan*	KINGDOM: ANIMALIA
		PHYLUM: CHORDATA
		CLASS: MAMMALIA
2 MONTHS	*Age when mothers regurgitate blood into a pup's (baby's) mouth*	ORDER: CHIROPTERA
		FAMILY: PHYLLOSTOMIDAE
		GENUS: DESMODUS
		SPECIES: D. ROTUNDUS
2 OUNCES	*Weight before a feeding*	

EGYPTIAN FRUIT BAT

Rousettus aegyptiacusfood

CONSERVATION STATUS: LEAST CONCERN

Egyptian fruit bats are known for their fox (or doglike) face and their dark brown to grayish-brown sleek fur. They live in many countries scattered across North Africa, sub-Saharan Africa, West Asia, and South Asia. They typically live in herds called a "roost" and dwell in caves, ruins, trees, old mines, and other abandoned locations. Egyptian fruit bats are frugivores, which means that they eat the pulp and juice from fruit. They provide essential roles in the ecosystems where they live. They pollinate many fruit trees, drawn to the flowers' sweet pollen scent, as they fly looking for more fruit. Egyptian fruit bats also play a prominent role in the seed disbursement of the baobab tree by eating the fruit and spitting, or pooping the seeds out and allowing seeds to spread and grow in new areas.

BY THE NUMBERS		CLASSIFICATION
50%–150% POUNDS	Amount of food eaten daily, relative to body weight	**KINGDOM:** ANIMALIA **PHYLUM:** CHORDATA **CLASS:** MAMMALIA **ORDER:** CHIROPTERA **FAMILY:** PTEROPODIDAE **GENUS:** ROUSETTUS **SPECIES:** R. AEGYPTIACUS
12 MILES	Distance it will travel for food	
24 INCHES	Wingspan	

GREATER HORSESHOE BAT *Rhinolophus ferrumequinum*

CONSERVATION STATUS: LEAST CONCERN

One of the most common identifying traits of greater horseshoe bats is the noseleaf—a fleshy, leaf-shaped structure on their nose. The top of the nose comes to a point, while the bottom of the nose is rounded in a horseshoe shape. Their nose is used for echolocation, a process in which echoes from noises bounce off objects to help guide flight. Greater horseshoe bats hibernate from October until April, when they will hang upside down from their feet and wrap their body in their membrane wings.

BY THE NUMBERS	
30 YEARS	Oldest recorded age of a greater horseshoe bat in the wild
6–10 DAYS	How often the bat awakes to hunt during hibernation
37.4 MILES	Average distance of echolocation pulse

CLASSIFICATION

KINGDOM: ANIMALIA
PHYLUM: CHORDATA
CLASS: MAMMALIA
ORDER: CHIROPTERA
FAMILY: RHINOLOPHIDAE
GENUS: RHINOLOPHUS
SPECIES: R. FERRUMEQUINUM

NIGHTLY FEAST

Greater horseshoe bats are insectivores and eat insects such as moths, beetles, butterflies, and cave spiders. They hunt at nightfall and fly close to the ground to catch their prey.

BISMARCK MASKED FLYING FOX *Pteropus capistratus*

CONSERVATION STATUS: VULNERABLE

Bismarck masked flying foxes are native to Papua New Guinea. They are named after the Bismarck Archipelago, a group of islands near New Guinea. One of their most unique characteristics is the males' ability to lactate (produce milk). They usually live alone and sleep on roosts or in nests. Their diet consists of fruit and plant matter.

BY THE NUMBERS	
4.3–4.6 INCHES	Forearm length
0–3,937 FEET	Elevation range
9,000–10,000	Number of mature individuals remaining

CLASSIFICATION	
KINGDOM:	ANIMALIA
PHYLUM:	CHORDATA
CLASS:	MAMMALIA
ORDER:	CHIROPTERA
FAMILY:	PTEROPODIDAE
GENUS:	PTEROPUS
SPECIES:	P. CAPISTRATUS

FLEETING FOXES

Sadly, there are fewer than 10,000 living adults left, and their numbers continue to shrink as their habitat declines.

CERVIDAE

Deer

The Cervidae family consists of hoofed, ruminant animals. Their distinguishing characteristic is their antlers, which they shed each year. Deer live in woodlands, tundra, and even tropical rainforests.

ESTIMATED NUMBER OF CERVIDAE SPECIES	55
DID YOU KNOW?	*In Old and Middle English, the word "deer" was used to describe any kind of wild animal. It wasn't until 1500 CE that the term took on the meaning it has today.*

CERVIDAE
Deer

CAPREOLINAE
New World Deer

CERVINAE
Old World Deer

RANGIFERINI
Reindeer, American Red Brocket, White-Tailed Deer, Mule Deer, Marsh Deer, Southern Pudu & Taruca

ALCEINI
Moose

MUNTIACINI
Reeve's Muntjac & Tufted Deer

CAPREOLINI
Water Deer & Roe Deer

CERVINI
Common Fallow Deer, Persian Fallow Deer, Rusa, Sumbar, Red Deer, Thorold's Deer, Skia Deer, Elk, Eld's Deer, Barasingha, Indian Hog Deer & Chital

NORTHERN PUDU *Pudu mephistophiles*

CONSERVATION STATUS: DECREASING

Northern pudus are the smallest species of deer in the world. They are crepuscular, meaning they are most active at twilight periods of the day—morning and late afternoon or early evening. They live alone and mark their territory with large piles of dung. They are shy, cautious animals and easily frightened. When spooked, the pudu will bark and its fur will bristle or shiver. Pudus are swift and run in zigzag paths when being chased. They can also climb and jump to escape predators if needed.

BY THE NUMBERS		CLASSIFICATION
13 POUNDS	Average weight	KINGDOM: Animalia
14–18 INCHES	Height	PHYLUM: Chordata
		CLASS: Mammalia
		ORDER: Artiodactyla
		FAMILY: Cervidae
40–62 ACRES	Individual territory	SUBFAMILY: Capreolinae
		GENUS: Pudu
		SPECIES: P. mephistophiles

PUDU FOOD

Male pudu get tree bark to eat with their antlers, while females use their teeth to chew it off.

FALLOW FASHION

Most fallow deer have spotted coats, but some herds have coats that are completely white or black.

EUROPEAN FALLOW DEER *Dama dama*

CONSERVATION STATUS: LEAST CONCERN

Adult European fallow deer have the same appearance as fawns, with white spots on the sides of their body. Their backside is white with black outlining either side, and they have a black stripe down their tail, which gives the appearance of a black number "111." Males, also called bucks, grow large and impressive antlers that are flat, not rounded. The antlers are palmate shaped, which means they look like an open palm of the hand with fingers extended. Bucks usually shed their antlers each year in April, and new antlers grow in by August.

BY THE NUMBERS	
31 MPH	Top speed
27 FEET	Length of antlers
4–6 CENTIMETERS	Length of hoofprint

CLASSIFICATION
KINGDOM: ANIMALIA
PHYLUM: CHORDATA
CLASS: MAMMALIA
ORDER: ARTIODACTYLA
FAMILY: CERVIDAE
SUBFAMILY: CERVINAE
TRIBE: CERVINI
GENUS: DAMA
SPECIES: D. DAMA

MOOSE *Alces alces*

CONSERVATION STATUS: LEAST CONCERN

Perhaps no North American animal is quite as impressive up close as a fully antlered bull moose. Moose are the largest members of the deer family and are often six to seven feet tall at the shoulders. Including the head and antlers, they can tower ten feet high, stretch eight to ten feet in length, and weigh up to 1,800 pounds—in other words, they're huge! With a long, homely face and a droopy upper lip, a moose's face looks rather like a horse's (although they're not related). These animals don't mind the cold, even extreme cold, though they do get hot and bothered by warm temperatures. Since moose easily overheat, their range is limited to colder, more northerly places.

BY THE NUMBERS

1 INCH PER DAY	*Speed that bull moose antlers can grow*
70 POUNDS	*Amount of food moose can consume each day during the plentiful summer months*
6 FEET	*Spread (or width) of a large set of moose antlers*

CLASSIFICATION

KINGDOM: ANIMALIA
PHYLUM: CHORDATA
CLASS: MAMMALIA
ORDER: ARTIODACTYLA
FAMILY: CERVIDAE
SUBFAMILY: CAPREOLINAE
TRIBE: ALCEINI
GENUS: ALCES
SPECIES: A. ALCES

WILD MOOSE CHASE

Since they have such long, lanky legs, moose appear to be walking on stilts, giving them a clumsy appearance. But don't be fooled—they can run up to thirty-five miles per hour and can easily run you down.

REINDEER AND CARIBOU *Rangifer tarandus*

CONSERVATION STATUS: LEAST CONCERN

Caribou and reindeer are the deer family's cold-weather specialists and are actually both subspecies of the species Rangifer tarandus. However, there are differences between the two animals. Caribou must travel to find food, and since food is scarce in the far north, they might need to journey 3,000 miles each year. Reindeer were domesticated many years ago and are still raised for their milk, meat, hides, and antlers. People also use them as draft animals to pull sleds.

BY THE NUMBERS

25% — *Reindeer noses have 25% more tiny blood vessels than human noses. This helps warm the frosty air as it's breathed in and makes all reindeer "red-nosed reindeer."*

4 YEARS — *The average lifespan of a male is four years less than that of a female.*

50 MPH — *Maximum speed of a reindeer—they're fast.*

CLASSIFICATION

KINGDOM: ANIMALIA
PHYLUM: CHORDATA
CLASS: MAMMALIA
ORDER: ARTIODACTYLA
FAMILY: CERVIDAE
SUBFAMILY: CAPREOLINAE
TRIBE: ODOCOILEINI
GENUS: RANGIFER
SPECIES: R. TARANDUS

RUDOLPH RAMPAGE

Reindeer and caribou reside in the far North and love to live in herds. Usually, there are just 10 to 100 of them, but when traveling they can form superherds of 50,000 to 500,000 animals—that's a lot of Rudolphs!

SUIDAE

Pigs and Boars

The biological Suidae family is made up of pigs and boars. Animals in this family all have a snout that ends in a rounded cartilage disk.

ESTIMATED NUMBER OF SUIDAE SPECIES	19
DID YOU KNOW?	*Pigs are so closely associated with humans that we have several words for them: the words "pig," "pork," and "swine" all have different roots.*

SUIDAE
Pigs and Boars

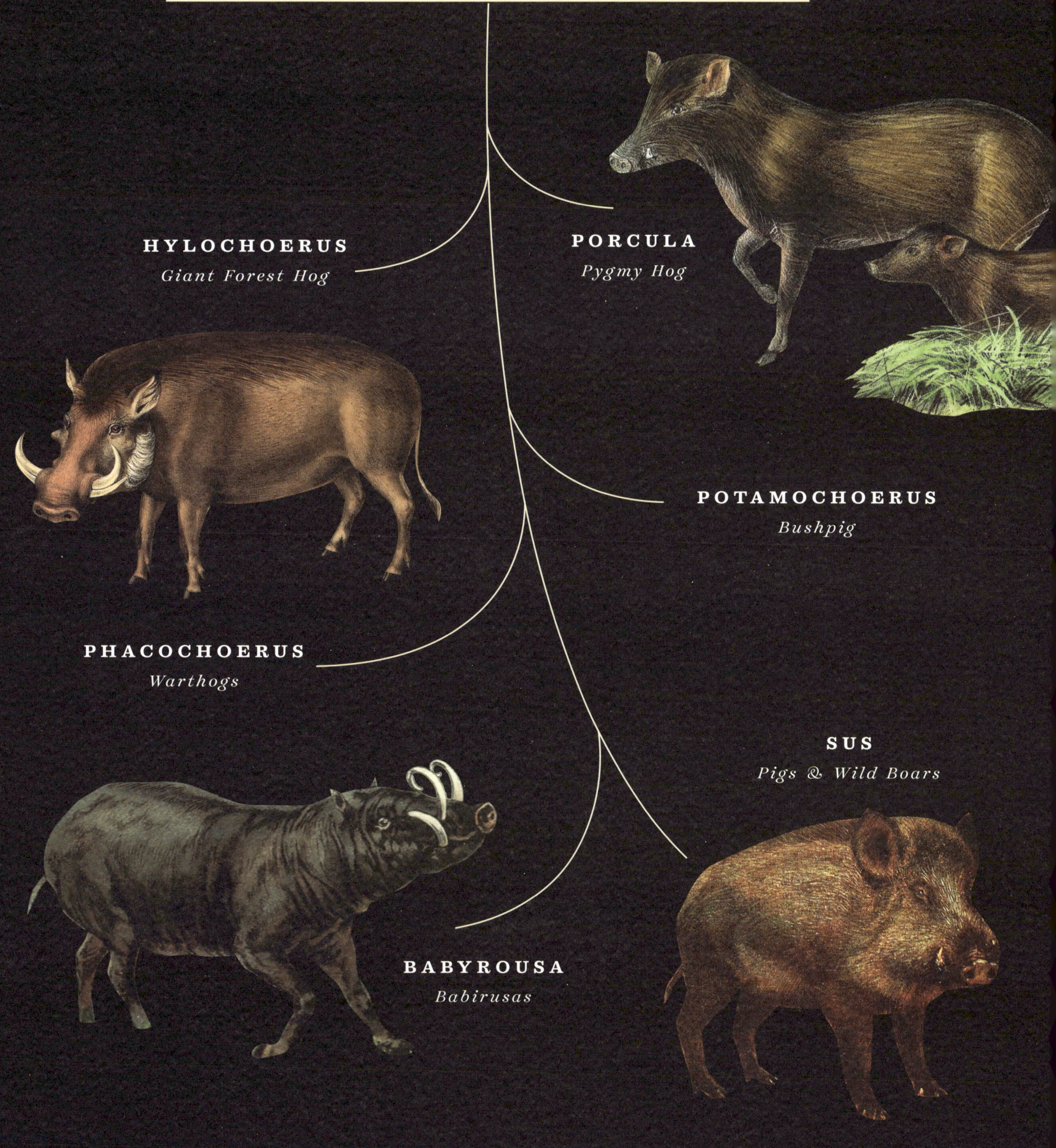

HYLOCHOERUS
Giant Forest Hog

PORCULA
Pygmy Hog

POTAMOCHOERUS
Bushpig

PHACOCHOERUS
Warthogs

SUS
Pigs & Wild Boars

BABYROUSA
Babirusas

INDIAN BOAR *Sus scrofa cristatus*

CONSERVATION STATUS: LEAST CONCERN

Indian boars are commonly referred to as Andamanese pigs or Moupin pigs. Indian boars usually live in groups called sounders that consist of 6–20 females, also known as sows. Males do not live in the sounders, except during mating. Male piglets stay with their mother until they have reached maturity at 1–2 years old; then they go off on their own. Mature females tend to stay in the same sounder as their mother. If a sounder becomes too large, smaller populations will break off into new groups.

BY THE NUMBERS	
4–6	*Piglets per litter*
2–4 INCHES	*Length of upper canine teeth*
600 POUNDS	*Maximum weight*

CLASSIFICATION	
KINGDOM:	ANIMALIA
PHYLUM:	CHORDATA
CLASS:	MAMMALIA
ORDER:	ARTIODACTYLA
FAMILY:	SUIDAE
GENUS:	SUS
SPECIES:	S. SCROFA
SUBSPECIES:	S. S. CRISTATUS

SMORGASBOARD

Indian boars are omnivorous, and its diet of plants and animals changes frequently based on availability, weather, and seasons.

CENTRAL EUROPEAN BOAR *Sus scrofa scrofa*

CONSERVATION STATUS: LEAST CONCERN

Central European boars rely heavily on their long, straight snout that is excellent for smelling. The boar's snout consists of a cartilaginous disk at the end, supported by a small bone called a prenasal. This design allows the snout to be used as a bulldozer of sorts, as the boar uses it to dig in the earth to search for food. Central European boars have small eyes and poor eyesight but a great sense of smell. They are found throughout Europe, with the exception of parts of Scandinavia, Greece, and Russia.

BY THE NUMBERS	
37 INCHES	*Maximum shoulder height*
2 WEEKS	*Age piglets begin to leave the nest for feedings*
7 MONTHS	*Age of independence*

CLASSIFICATION	
KINGDOM:	Animalia
PHYLUM:	Chordata
CLASS:	Mammalia
ORDER:	Artiodactyla
FAMILY:	Suidae
GENUS:	Sus
SPECIES:	S. scrofa
SUBSPECIES:	S. s. scrofa

WHEN PIGS SWIM

In addition to their terrific sense of smell, Central European boars are great swimmers!

WARTHOG *Phacochoerus*

CONSERVATION STATUS: LEAST CONCERN

Warthogs have very little fat and a sparse coat, which makes them very susceptible to the sun and cold. In the summer months, warthogs roll in water or mud to cool themselves down. The mud also provides an extra layer of protection from the sun. During the winter, warthogs huddle together, using body heat for warmth while sheltering in burrows. Warthogs have a mutualistic relationship (a relationship where two different species "work together" and each gains something in return) with red- and yellow-billed oxpeckers. The oxpeckers sit on the warthog's back and enjoy a tasty meal of ticks and parasites. In return, the warthog is rid of the parasites.

BY THE NUMBERS	
35 MPH	*Top speed*
3	*Piglets per litter*
50%	*Survival rate in the first year of life*

CLASSIFICATION	
KINGDOM:	Animalia
PHYLUM:	Chordata
CLASS:	Mammalia
ORDER:	Artiodactyla
FAMILY:	Suidae
GENUS:	Phacochoerus
SPECIES:	P. africanus

PYGMY HOG *Porcula salvania*

CONSERVATION STATUS: ENDANGERED

The pygmy hog is known for being the smallest and rarest wild hog in the world. It is one of the few mammals that builds a home, or nest, by digging a shallow hole in the ground. The pygmy hog lines the hole with grass for soft bedding, adding branches to create a small roof to shade and protect the nest. They use these nests to rest and regulate their body temperature from the heat of the day and to keep warm during the winter. Pygmy hogs are native to the Himalayas in northern India, Bhutan, and Nepal, but now can only be found in Assam, India. They are considered an endangered species as much of their dense grasslands habitat has been eliminated.

BY THE NUMBERS	
18 POUNDS	*Average weight*
10 INCHES	*Shoulder height*
6–10 HOURS	*Daily foraging*

CLASSIFICATION
KINGDOM: ANIMALIA
PHYLUM: CHORDATA
CLASS: MAMMALIA
ORDER: ARTIODACTYLA
FAMILY: SUIDAE
SUBFAMILY: SUINAE
GENUS: PORCULA
SPECIES: P. SALVANIA

EQUUS

Horses, Donkeys, and Zebras

The Equus genus consists of horses, donkeys, and zebras.

ESTIMATED NUMBER OF EQUUS SPECIES 7

DID YOU KNOW? Horses and their kin originated in North America, but all wild species have been extinct there for 12,000 years.

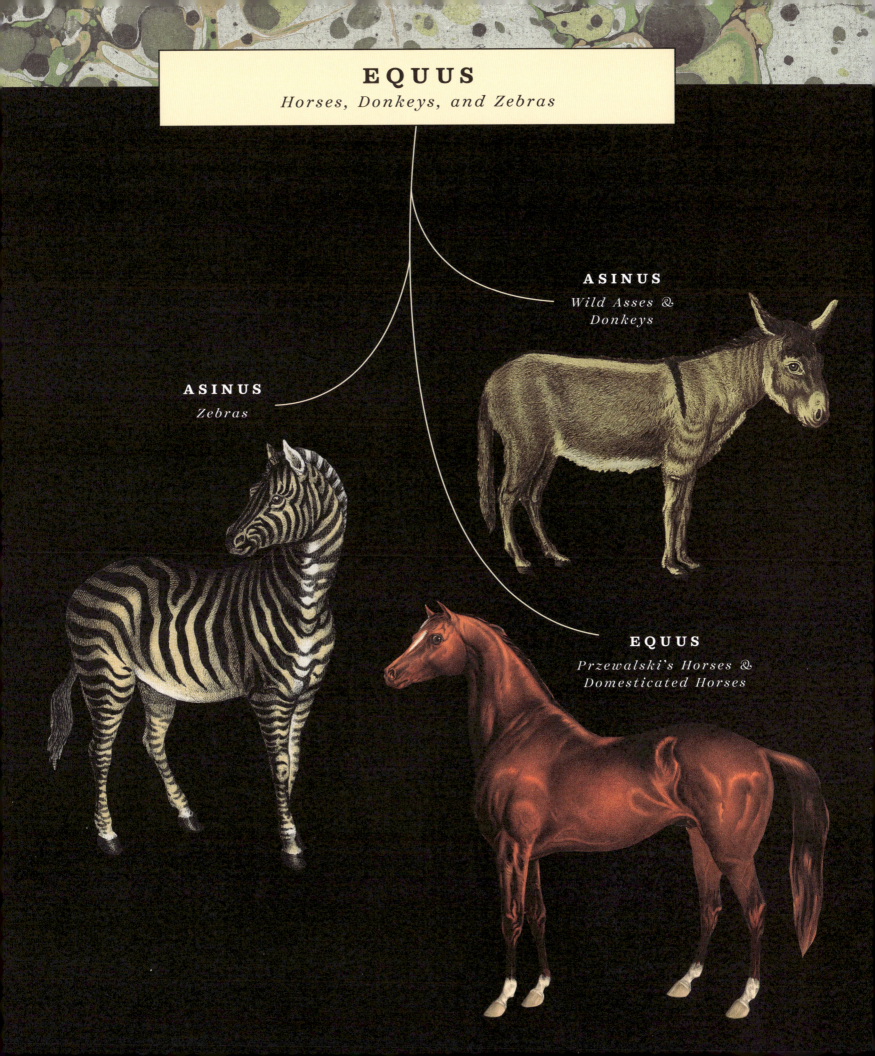

PLAINS ZEBRA *Equus quagga*

CONSERVATION STATUS: NEAR THREATENED

The Plains zebra is easily identified by its bold, black-and-white stripe pattern, which begins with vertical stripes at the head and ends with horizontal stripes near the tail. The stripes along the side of its body are connected all the way to its stomach. This stripe pattern also reflects the heat from the sun and acts as camouflage against predators. Plains zebras are grazing mammals and typically are the first species to arrive in a new grazing area, where they prefer to feed on the coarser top grass. They depend on fresh water for survival and will travel great distances each year to follow the rains.

BY THE NUMBERS	
70%	Amount of heat reflected by their stripe pattern from the sun
300 MILES	Annual rain migration
15 MILES	Distance from a water source at any given time

CLASSIFICATION

KINGDOM: Animalia
PHYLUM: Chordata
CLASS: Mammalia
ORDER: Perissodactyla
FAMILY: Equidae
GENUS: Equus
SUBGENUS: Hippotigris
SPECIES: E. quagga

ONE OF A KIND

Each zebra has a unique stripe pattern, so no two individuals look alike—similar to a human's fingerprints.

ONAGER *Equus hemionus*

CONSERVATION STATUS: NEAR THREATENED

The onager is a wild ass or donkey species. It is characterized by a sandy-red-colored coat and a dark brown dorsal stripe down its spine, which is surrounded by white strips and continues down its tail and rump. The flanks and belly of the onager are also white. Its coat is not waterproof, so onagers avoid being out in the rain as it is hazardous for their health. Onagers live in herds that usually contain one male (stallion) and multiple females with their foals. Older stallions typically live alone; however, in some rare situations, it has been noted that small herds of just males will unite for protection against predators.

BY THE NUMBERS	
10–12	Herd size
1 YEAR	Gestation (pregnancy) period
2 YEARS	How long a foal stays with its mother

CLASSIFICATION
KINGDOM: ANIMALIA
PHYLUM: CHORDATA
CLASS: MAMMALIA
ORDER: PERISSODACTYLA
FAMILY: EQUIDAE
GENUS: EQUUS
SUBGENUS: ASINUS
SPECIES: E. HEMIONUS

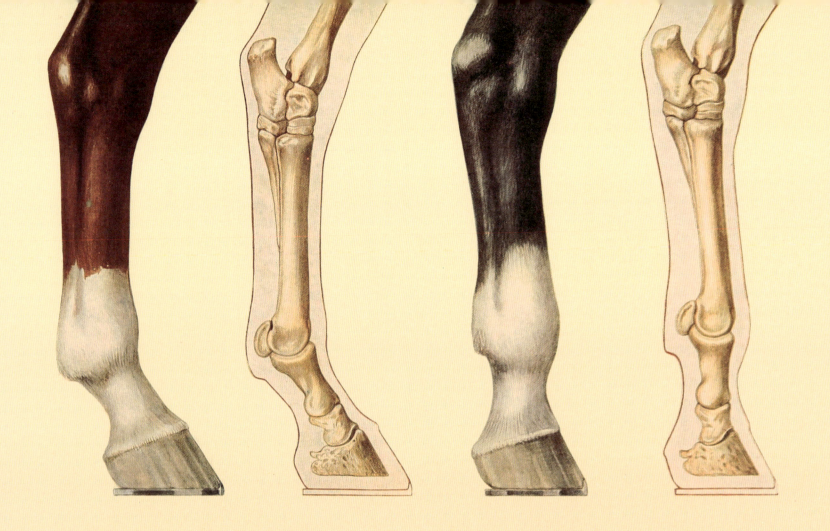

HORSE *Equus ferus caballus*

CONSERVATION STATUS: LEAST CONCERN

The relationship between humans and horses goes back for thousands of years. Humans first domesticated horses around 6,000 years ago, and they've been among our staunchest friends and closest allies ever since. These animals, more than any other, have been at the center of human progress. They've carried us, worked for us, fought for us, and died for us. They've impacted our culture in countless ways—in stories, books, songs, movies, and even in language. You know many horsy sayings like, "Don't look a gift horse in the mouth," "horseplay," "Hold your horses," and "Get off your high horse," to name just a few. Even today, when horses are no longer necessary for pulling our carts or fighting with us in our battles, there remains a deep spiritual bond between people and their horses and that will never change.

BY THE NUMBERS	
60 MILLION	Estimated number of horses worldwide
3 HOURS	Average time horses sleep each day, mostly in naps while standing
10 GALLONS	Amount of saliva a typical horse produces each day; an average human makes only 0.19 gallons

CLASSIFICATION
KINGDOM: ANIMALIA
PHYLUM: CHORDATA
CLASS: MAMMALIA
ORDER: PERISSODACTYLA
FAMILY: EQUIDAE
GENUS: EQUUS
SPECIES: E. FERUS
SUBSPECIES: E. F. CABALLUS

DONKEY *Equus africanus asinus*

BRAINIACS

Compared to horses, donkeys might have a reputation for being more stubborn, yet donkeys have nothing to be ashamed of. They're quite intelligent. That legendary stubbornness? It's really just the donkey being smart. A donkey considers any command carefully and refuses to do anything it thinks is dangerous.

CONSERVATION STATUS: LEAST CONCERN

Donkeys are the underappreciated cousins of horses. Also known as burros or jackasses, donkeys are descended from the wild ass of north Africa. Today, wild donkeys live in the American Southwest. Donkeys are a lot tougher than horses. They're sturdier, stronger pound-for-pound, require less food and water, and live longer. Horses are flight animals and will bolt if startled, whereas donkeys are not easily panicked. They'll stand their ground and fight.

BY THE NUMBERS

25 YEARS	Amount of time a donkey can remember people, places, and other donkeys
95%	Percentage of its food a typical donkey can digest and use, meaning donkey manure is not a good fertilizer
50+ YEARS	Typical lifespan of a donkey—they can live for a long time!

CLASSIFICATION

KINGDOM: Animalia
PHYLUM: Chordata
CLASS: Mammalia
ORDER: Perissodactyla
FAMILY: Equidae
GENUS: Equus
SPECIES: E. africanus
SUBSPECIES: E. a. asinus

QUAGGA *Equus quagga quagga*

CONSERVATION STATUS: EXTINCT

Quaggas were native to Southern Africa and lived in the Karoo regions of Cape Province and South Africa. They lived in arid to temperate grasslands and ate tall grasses. The quagga was once believed to be a separate species of zebra; however, after analyzing DNA, scientists concluded that the quagga was a subspecies of the Plains zebra. Before becoming extinct, the quagga was recognized by its sandy-brown coat, white tail, and black stripes only on the upper part of its body. The spacing of the stripes became wider in the middle part of the body until the stripes faded altogether.

BY THE NUMBERS

11 SQUARE MILES	*Home range*
1870s	*Last remaining wild quagga was killed*
500–700 POUNDS	*Weight*

CLASSIFICATION

- **KINGDOM:** Animalia
- **PHYLUM:** Chordata
- **CLASS:** Mammalia
- **ORDER:** Perissodactyla
- **FAMILY:** Equidae
- **GENUS:** Equus
- **SPECIES:** E. quagga
- **SUBSPECIES:** E. q. quagga

LOST ZEBRA

In the 1800s, quaggas were hunted for their meat and hide, which led to their ultimate extinction.

RODENTIA

Rodents

Rodents are part of their own mammalian order called Rodentia, which is derived from the Latin word *rodere*, meaning "to gnaw." This name is fitting, as animals in this group all have incisor teeth on the upper and lower jaw that never stop growing.

ESTIMATED NUMBER OF RODENTIA SPECIES

2,277

DID YOU KNOW? *Rodents are extremely versatile and participate in every biological niche imaginable. They can be herbivores and carnivores, nocturnal or diurnal, and solitary or communal.*

RODENTIA
Rodents

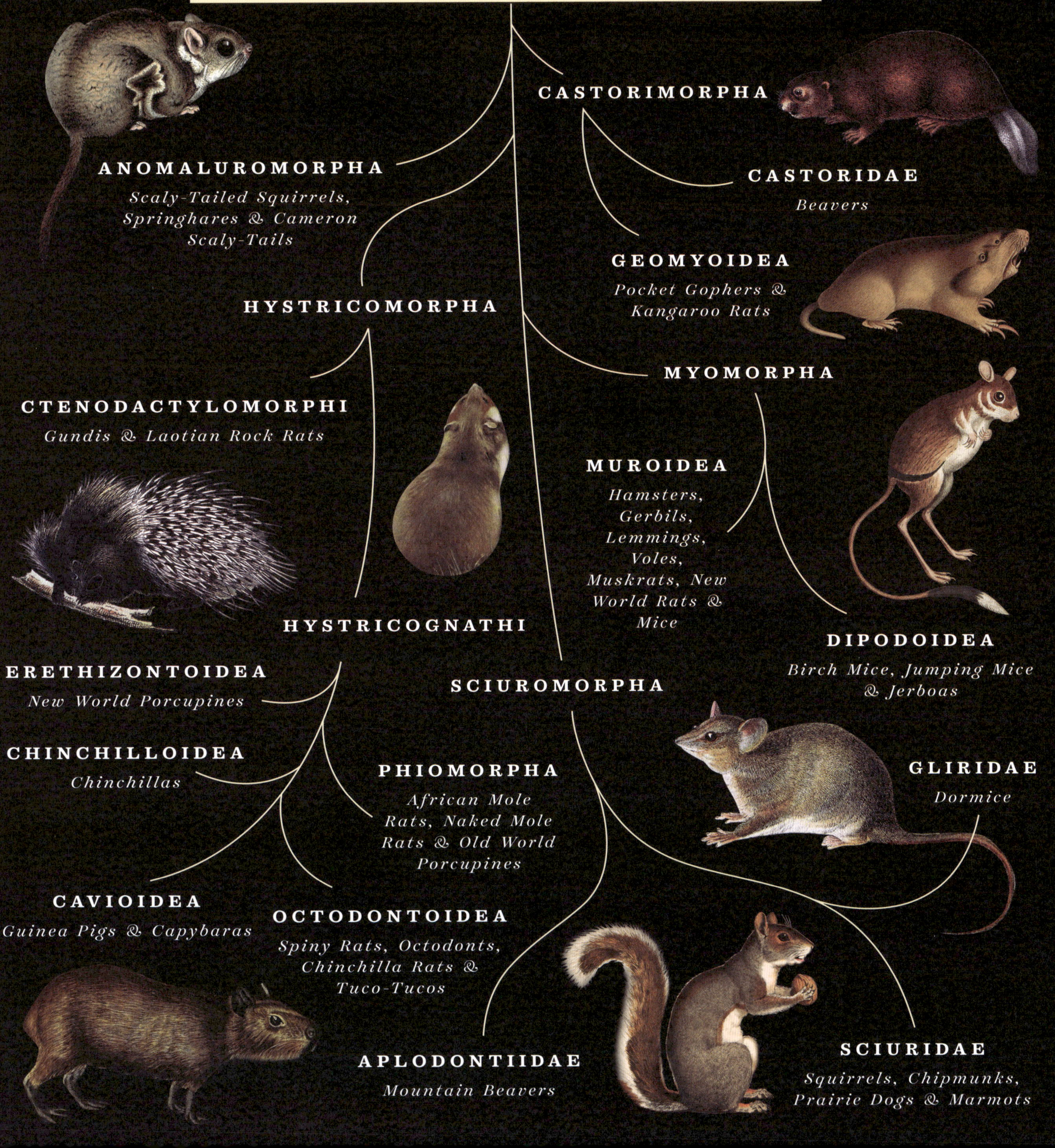

CASTORIMORPHA

ANOMALUROMORPHA
Scaly-Tailed Squirrels, Springhares & Cameron Scaly-Tails

CASTORIDAE
Beavers

GEOMYOIDEA
Pocket Gophers & Kangaroo Rats

HYSTRICOMORPHA

MYOMORPHA

CTENODACTYLOMORPHI
Gundis & Laotian Rock Rats

MUROIDEA
Hamsters, Gerbils, Lemmings, Voles, Muskrats, New World Rats & Mice

DIPODOIDEA
Birch Mice, Jumping Mice & Jerboas

HYSTRICOGNATHI

SCIUROMORPHA

ERETHIZONTOIDEA
New World Porcupines

CHINCHILLOIDEA
Chinchillas

PHIOMORPHA
African Mole Rats, Naked Mole Rats & Old World Porcupines

GLIRIDAE
Dormice

CAVIOIDEA
Guinea Pigs & Capybaras

OCTODONTOIDEA
Spiny Rats, Octodonts, Chinchilla Rats & Tuco-Tucos

APLODONTIIDAE
Mountain Beavers

SCIURIDAE
Squirrels, Chipmunks, Prairie Dogs & Marmots

CRESTED PORCUPINE *Hystrix cristata*

CONSERVATION STATUS: LEAST CONCERN

Crested porcupines are covered in black-and-white quills that vary in length depending on the location on their body. The quills usually lay flat; however, if threatened or angered, porcupines will raise their quills, forming a crest shape. This is a defense mechanism and scares predators into thinking that they are larger than they actually are. Crested porcupines take shelter by digging burrows into the earth using their front feet. The burrows can be elaborate, as crested porcupines share them with family and use their burrows for many years.

BY THE NUMBERS	
1–13 INCHES	Quill length
9 MILES	Daily foraging distance
3–6.5 INCHES	Tail length

CLASSIFICATION	
KINGDOM:	ANIMALIA
PHYLUM:	CHORDATA
CLASS:	MAMMALIA
ORDER:	RODENTIA
FAMILY:	HYSTRICIDAE
GENUS:	HYSTRIX
SPECIES:	H. CRISTATA

PORCUPINE POINTS

Crested porcupines may also stomp their feet, click their teeth, and rattle their quills to scare predators away.

DOMESTIC GUINEA PIG *Cavia porcellus*

CONSERVATION STATUS: NOT EVALUATED

Guinea pigs, also known as cavies, have no relation to pigs at all and are actually members of the rodent family. The name "guinea pig" is believed to have come from an old English coin called a "guinea," as well as from their squealing sound, which resembles that of a pig. At the time, guinea pigs were expensive and they each cost one guinea, so the name "guinea pig" meant "the little pig that cost a guinea." The domestication of guinea pigs began in South America. It is believed that Spanish explorers later brought guinea pigs home to Europe after their expedition in the Andes, where they were kept as exotic pets. Further colonization of South America by the Europeans spread guinea pigs throughout the world, and it is now a global pet.

BY THE NUMBERS	
20	Coat colors and combinations
13	Coat textures and lengths
7,000 YEARS AGO	Beginning of domestication

CLASSIFICATION

KINGDOM: ANIMALIA
PHYLUM: CHORDATA
CLASS: MAMMALIA
ORDER: RODENTIA
FAMILY: CAVIIDAE
GENUS: CAVIA
SPECIES: C. PORCELLUS

NORTHERN FLYING SQUIRREL *Glaucomys sabrinus*

CONSERVATION STATUS: LEAST CONCERN

Northern flying squirrels are one of the three species of New World flying squirrels. They are found in Canada and the United States in habitats dominated by conifer trees and deciduous forests.

BY THE NUMBERS	
8	Members living in a group
2 HOURS	Daily time spent foraging, at sunset and sunrise
65 FEET	Average gliding distance

CLASSIFICATION
KINGDOM: ANIMALIA
PHYLUM: CHORDATA
CLASS: MAMMALIA
ORDER: RODENTIA
FAMILY: SCIURIDAE
GENUS: GLAUCOMYS
SPECIES: G. SABRINUS

GREAT GLIDERS

Despite their name, northern flying squirrels do not fly—they glide. They have a special fold of skin called a patagia between their front and back legs. When they stretch their legs out, the patagia is pulled tight, creating a parachute effect. This allows the northern flying squirrel to gracefully glide from tree to tree.

EASTERN GRAY SQUIRREL *Sciurus carolinensis*

CONSERVATION STATUS: LEAST CONCERN

Eastern gray squirrels live primarily in the United States and Canada in dense forests of oaks, hickories, and walnuts, which provide plenty of food. They have a tremendous sense of smell that helps them locate food that they've hidden or buried. They are also able to learn information about other squirrels by smelling them, such as their stress levels and reproduction status.

BY THE NUMBERS	
2	Litters per year
2–4	Kits (babies) per litter
0.5 OUNCES	Birth weight

CLASSIFICATION
KINGDOM: ANIMALIA
PHYLUM: CHORDATA
CLASS: MAMMALIA
ORDER: RODENTIA
FAMILY: SCIURIDAE
GENUS: SCIURUS
SPECIES: S. CAROLINENSIS

SQUIRREL SIGNALS

Eastern gray squirrels are very good at communicating with other squirrels, using tail twitching, facial expression, or their posture. They also use different sounds to warn others of approaching predators, to announce when a predator has left, or to show affection with one another.

INDIAN GIANT SQUIRREL *Ratufa indica*

CONSERVATION STATUS: LEAST CONCERN

Indian giant squirrels live in the rainforests of India and are commonly referred to as Malabar giant squirrels, or "rainbow squirrels." Indian giant squirrels spend almost all their time in trees. They can propel themselves great distances, jumping from one branch or tree to another. If a predator is near, such as a leopard, an eagle, or a snake, the squirrel will lie flat against the tree bark, hug the limb, and hold very still in order to blend in with the bark and avoid detection.

BY THE NUMBERS	
20 FEET	*Propelling distance*
2–3	*Common color patterns*
2.5 FEET	*Length*

CLASSIFICATION
KINGDOM: ANIMALIA
PHYLUM: CHORDATA
CLASS: MAMMALIA
ORDER: RODENTIA
FAMILY: SCIURIDAE
GENUS: RATUFA
SPECIES: R. INDICA

THE HIGH LIFE

Indian giant squirrels construct large nests out of twigs and leaves in the tree canopies, where they store their food. They typically only come out of the trees to chase each other during mating season.

DAM DWELLING

The beaver family home is the beaver lodge, a large, dome-shaped structure that's very sturdy—even a grizzly can't break in. It has two underwater entrances, like a front and back door. Inside, there's a raised platform, well off the water, that's covered with bark, grass, and wood shavings. It all makes for a comfy-cozy dwelling, especially during winter.

AMERICAN BEAVER *Castor canadensis*

CONSERVATION STATUS: LEAST CONCERN

The beaver is a famously busy semiaquatic rodent. It has webbed hind feet and a flat tail, which it employs like a rudder. Also, a beaver comes equipped with see-through inner eyelids that act like swim goggles. Since it's rather clumsy on land, it needs deep water for protection. So, if a pond or lake isn't handy, it will make one by damming a river or stream with a dam made from logs, branches, or stones—whatever's handy. Beavers mate for life and form unusually strong family units.

BY THE NUMBERS

15 MINUTES	Maximum amount of time that beavers can stay underwater without surfacing
110 YARDS	The typical width of a beaver dam (about the length of a football field), with the largest on record measuring over a mile wide
1 INCH	Length of the four beaver incisors (front teeth)

CLASSIFICATION

KINGDOM: ANIMALIA
PHYLUM: CHORDATA
CLASS: MAMMALIA
ORDER: RODENTIA
FAMILY: CASTORIDAE
GENUS: CASTOR
SPECIES: C. CANADENSIS

DESERT KANGAROO RAT *Dipodomys deserti*

CONSERVATION STATUS: LEAST CONCERN

Desert kangaroo rats live in underground burrows in southwestern North America, primarily in sand dunes or desert areas. They are light brown or gray in color with a white belly. Desert kangaroo rats have long tails, big eyes, and a small nose and ears. They have a special cooling system in their nose and nasal passage that allows them to cool off without losing necessary moisture from their body. When a desert kangaroo rat approaches an unknown object, it will kick dirt on it to see if the object is a possible threat or predator. If the object doesn't react, they know they are safe.

BY THE NUMBERS	
9 FEET	Jumping distance
5.5–8 YEARS	Life expectancy in captivity
4	Number of toes on their large hind feet

CLASSIFICATION	
KINGDOM:	Animalia
PHYLUM:	Chordata
CLASS:	Mammalia
ORDER:	Rodentia
FAMILY:	Heteromyidae
GENUS:	Dipodomys
SPECIES:	D. deserti

NORTHERN POCKET GOPHER *Thomomys talpoides*

CONSERVATION STATUS: LEAST CONCERN

Northern pocket gophers have thick, tapered bodies with outer cheek pockets used for storing food. They have short, soft, grayish-brown fur, short legs, strong claws, and sharp incisor teeth on both their upper and bottom jaw that they use for digging. Their lips can close behind their front four incisor teeth, preventing them from getting dirt in their mouths while they dig. Northern pocket gophers dig intricate tunnels and burrows below ground consisting of two distinct levels. The upper level, closest to the surface, is where feces are stored and the inner level is where they nest and store food. The tunnels are generally kept plugged with soil, but are occasionally aired out during periods of nice weather. Northern pocket gophers are herbivores that eat an array of roots, tubers, and aboveground plants and will pull their food underground into their burrows for consumption.

BY THE NUMBERS	
164 YARDS	Tunnel distance a single northern pocket gopher can dig
8 INCHES	Body length
2.5 INCHES	Tail length

CLASSIFICATION	
KINGDOM:	ANIMALIA
PHYLUM:	CHORDATA
CLASS:	MAMMALIA
ORDER:	RODENTIA
FAMILY:	GEOMYIDAE
GENUS:	THOMOMYS
SPECIES:	T. TALPOIDES

FAWN HOPPING MOUSE *Notomys cervinus*

CONSERVATION STATUS: NEAR THREATENED

Fawn hopping mice live in the arid regions of the Australian outback. They are sandy-brown or gray in color, with a white belly. They have very long tails and long back legs and feet, allowing them to hop quickly. Fawn hopping mice have long ears and large, protruding eyes. They are nocturnal creatures and live and sleep underground in simply made burrows that are shared with their family or group. Fawn hopping mice do not require fresh sources of water for survival because their bodies have the ability to tolerate large amounts of salt.

BY THE NUMBERS	
2–4	Group size
3 FEET	Burrowing depth
1–3	Openings in each burrow

CLASSIFICATION	
KINGDOM:	ANIMALIA
PHYLUM:	CHORDATA
CLASS:	MAMMALIA
ORDER:	RODENTIA
FAMILY:	MURIDAE
GENUS:	NOTOMYS
SPECIES:	N. CERVINUS

WOOD MOUSE *Apodemus sylvaticus*

CONSERVATION STATUS: LEAST CONCERN

Wood mice are small rodents, commonly called long-tailed field mice or European wood mice. They are gray or sandy brown in color, with a light gray or white belly. They have a long tail, with large ears and eyes. Their large eyes help them see at night, which allows for added protection against predators. They also have a very keen sense of smell. They can smell the exact location of buried food without having to randomly search for it.

BY THE NUMBERS	
21–26 DAYS	Gestation (pregnancy) period
4–7	Pups per litter
13 DAYS	For pups' eyes to open

CLASSIFICATION
KINGDOM: Animalia
PHYLUM: Chordata
CLASS: Mammalia
ORDER: Rodentia
FAMILY: Muridae
GENUS: Apodemus
SPECIES: A. sylvaticus

MARSUPIALIA

Marsupials

The Marsupialia infraclass is made up of mammals called marsupials: animals whose offspring are carried in an external pouch. Some well-known marsupials include kangaroos, koalas, and opossums.

ESTIMATED NUMBER OF MARSUPIALIA SPECIES 334

DID YOU KNOW? *Although marsupials are generally associated with Australia, DNA evidence shows that they originated in South America, where some still live today.*

MARSUPIALIA
Marsupials

- **AUSTRALIDELPHIA**
  - **MICROBIOTHERIA** — *Monitos del monte*
- **AMERIDELPHIA**
  - **DIDELPHIDAE** — *Opossums*
  - **CAENOLESTIDAE** — *Shrew Opossums*
- **DASYUROMORPHIA** — *Quolls, Dunnarts, Tasmanian Devils & Numbats*
- **DIPROTODONTIA**
  - **PHALANGERIFORMES** — *Pygmy Possums, Gliders, Ringtailed Possums & Cuscuses*
  - **PHALANGERIDA**
    - **MACROPODIFORMES** — *Kangaroos & Wallabies*
    - **VOMBATIFORMES**
      - **VOMBATIDAE** — *Wombats*
      - **PHASCOLARCTIDAE** — *Koalas*
- **PERAMELEMORPHIA** — *Bilbies & Bandicoots*
- **NOTORYCTEMORPHIA** — *Marsupial Moles*

TIGER QUOLL *Dasyurus maculatus*

CONSERVATION STATUS: NEAR THREATENED

Tiger quolls have a similar appearance to the mongoose. They are reddish-brown in color, with white spots all over their bodies and tail. They are carnivores, and their diet consists mainly of greater gliders, possums, rabbits, bandicoots, pademelons, birds, and rats. Tiger quolls share a common "latrine" site where they leave scat and their scent mark behind. Although tiger quolls typically live alone, the latrine site provides a sense of community and a place to gather information about one another from the scent they leave behind: They can keep track of relatives and establish dominance, and females advertise the start of mating season.

BY THE NUMBERS	
5	Pups per litter
7–8 POUNDS	Weight of a mature male
2–5 YEARS	Lifespan in the wild

CLASSIFICATION	
KINGDOM:	Animalia
PHYLUM:	Chordata
CLASS:	Mammalia
INFRACLASS:	Marsupialia
ORDER:	Dasyuromorphia
FAMILY:	Dasyuridae
GENUS:	Dasyurus
SPECIES:	D. maculatus

COARSE-HAIRED WOMBAT *Vombatus ursinus*

CONSERVATION STATUS: LEAST CONCERN

Coarse-haired wombats, also called common wombats, have stubby legs and a large, rounded body. Their eyes and ears are small, and they vary in color from tan, brown, gray, or black. They have sharp claws and constantly growing incisor teeth. Coarse-haired wombats are nicknamed "the bulldozers of the bush." They dig with their front feet and then push the dirt behind them with their rump, similar to a bulldozer.

BY THE NUMBERS	
16 HOURS	Amount of time spent sleeping daily
6 MONTHS	How long a joey (baby) stays in the mother's pouch
44–77 POUNDS	Weight

CLASSIFICATION

KINGDOM: ANIMALIA
PHYLUM: CHORDATA
CLASS: MAMMALIA
INFRACLASS: MARSUPIALIA
ORDER: DIPROTODONTIA
FAMILY: VOMBATIDAE
GENUS: VOMBATUS
SPECIES: V. URSINUS

COMMON BRUSHTAIL POSSUM *Trichosurus vulpecula*

CONSERVATION STATUS: LEAST CONCERN

Common brushtail possums have a variety of coat colors, including gray, brown, black, and reddish-gold. Each color variation has a lighter belly than the rest of their body. They have big eyes, long ears, and a long, bushy, prehensile tail that is used to grasp branches to support themselves in the tree canopy. They also have clawless first toes on their hind feet, which aid in the gripping of tree branches. Common brushtail possums have scent glands located near their chin, chest, and tail, which are used to mark their territory. They are herbivores, with their favorite food being eucalyptus flowers.

BY THE NUMBERS	
16–18 DAYS	*Gestational (pregnancy) period*
4–5 MONTHS	*How long a joey stays in its mother's pouch*
13–15 YEARS	*Lifespan in the wild*

CLASSIFICATION

- KINGDOM: Animalia
- PHYLUM: Chordata
- CLASS: Mammalia
- INFRACLASS: Marsupialia
- ORDER: Diprotodontia
- FAMILY: Phalangeridae
- GENUS: Trichosurus
- SPECIES: T. vulpecula

PUTRID PLAY

If really frightened, a possum will faint and "play dead"—lolling tongue, foamy drool, the works—from which we get the saying, "playing possum." However, the possum is not playing. It's actually in a catatonic state, like a deep sleep, to trick predators who often don't like to eat dead prey. The possum even releases a foul-smelling green liquid from its anal glands so it smells dead. Possum for dinner? Ah, no thanks.

VIRGINIA OPOSSUM *Didelphis virginiana*

CONSERVATION STATUS: LEAST CONCERN

The Virginia opossum, or "possum" for short, is North America's only marsupial. An opossum's paws are more like very nimble hands, each with five delicate, well-separated fingers. The big toe on each hind paw is actually an opposable thumb like on your hand. This helps possums grab branches. Also, a possum has a prehensile tail that can grab on to things. It's used like a fifth hand.

BY THE NUMBERS	
1/2 INCH	Length of a newborn opossum joey
4 HOURS	The maximum time a possum might be unconscious while "playing possum"
1/200 OF AN OUNCE	Weight of a newborn joey, about 1/10 the weight of a paperclip

CLASSIFICATION	
KINGDOM:	ANIMALIA
PHYLUM:	CHORDATA
CLASS:	MAMMALIA
INFRACLASS:	MARSUPIALIA
ORDER:	DIDELPHIMORPHIA
FAMILY:	DIDELPHIDAE
GENUS:	DIDELPHIS
SPECIES:	D. VIRGINIANA

CETACEA

Whales & Dolphins

The Cetacea infraorder consists of whales, dolphins, and porpoises. These are the only fully aquatic mammals.

ESTIMATED NUMBER OF CETACEA SPECIES	130
DID YOU KNOW?	*Cetaceans have been extensively hunted for their meat, blubber, and oil by both indigenous peoples and commercial operations.*

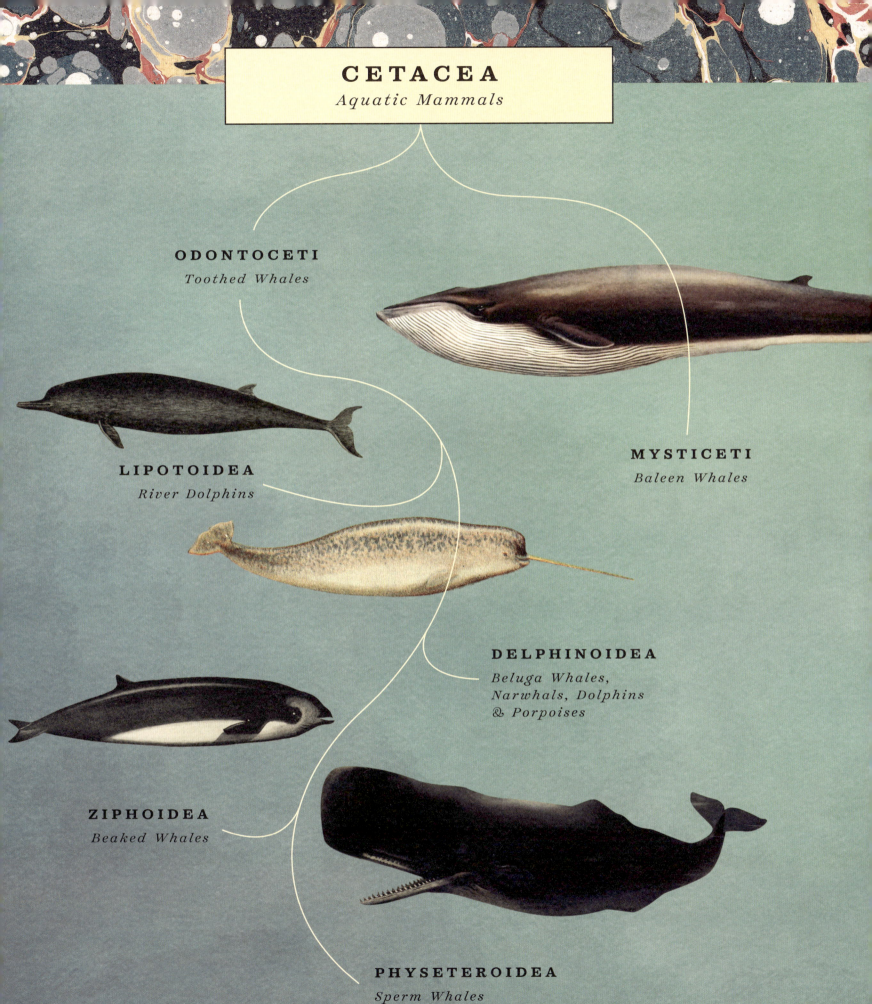

BLUE WHALE *Balaenoptera musculus*

CONSERVATION STATUS: ENDANGERED

Blue whales are the largest known animals to ever exist on earth. They are very long and slim, and grayish-blue in color. They have grooves on their throat and often have barnacles attached to their skin. Blue whales do not have teeth, but instead have baleen plates that filter out food from the sea water. They also have the deepest and loudest voice of any whale species. They can reach decibels of 188; comparably, a jet plane reaches 140 decibels.

BY THE NUMBERS

3–4 TONS	Amount of krill a blue whale can eat per day
80–100 FEET	Length
395	Number of baleen plates along the upper jaw

CLASSIFICATION

KINGDOM: ANIMALIA
PHYLUM: CHORDATA
CLASS: MAMMALIA
ORDER: ARTIODACTYLA
INFRAORDER: CETACEA
FAMILY: BALAENOPTERIDAE
GENUS: BALAENOPTERA
SPECIES: B. MUSCULUS

BOWHEAD WHALE *Balaena mysticetus*

CONSERVATION STATUS: LEAST CONCERN

The bowhead whale is the only whale with baleen to be found only in arctic waters. It's mouth makes up one-third of its total length, making it the largest mouth of any animal! Bowhead whales tend to travel alone, though they can sometimes be found in small groups called pods. Like other baleen whales, their main source of food is krill and other zooplankton. Amazingly, bowhead whales can live for more than 200 years!

BY THE NUMBERS	
268 YEARS	*Maximum expected lifespan, though they usually live shorter lives in the wild*
500 FEET	*Depth a bowhead whale can reach when diving*
17–19 INCHES	*Thickness of blubber*

CLASSIFICATION

- KINGDOM: ANIMALIA
- PHYLUM: CHORDATA
- CLASS: MAMMALIA
- ORDER: ARTIODACTYLA
- INFRAORDER: CETACEA
- FAMILY: BALAENIDAE
- GENUS: BALAENA
- SPECIES: B. MYSTICETUS

HOW BALEEN WORKS

Baleen is a strong and flexible substance made from keratin and shaped into plates fringed with stiff hairs. The plates hang down from the upper jaw like a curtain, making the perfect filter. When a whale spots a school of krill, she accelerates and lunges, mouth open. As she does, thousands of gallons of krill-filled water get pushed into her mouth, inflating her feeding sac. The whale closes her mouth, uses her tongue to push out the water through her baleen, and the krill stay behind. Gulp!

SPERM WHALE *Physeter macrocephalus*

CONSERVATION STATUS: VULNERABLE

Sperm whales are gray, with some that have white patches on their belly. They have small paddle-shaped flippers, and their blowhole is S-shaped and sits off-center on the left side of their head. Sperm whales are sociable mammals that typically live in groups. These groups are usually determined upon age and sex. Sperm whales are most identifiable by their large heads, which contain the spermaceti organ. This organ contains a waxy substance that is believed to be a cooling and heating agent to assist with volume and buoyancy during prolonged dives.

BY THE NUMBERS	
30	Average number of sperm whales in a pod
2,000 FEET	Diving depth
45 MINUTES	Duration of dive

CLASSIFICATION

KINGDOM: ANIMALIA
PHYLUM: CHORDATA
CLASS: MAMMALIA
ORDER: ARTIODACTYLA
INFRAORDER: CETACEA
FAMILY: PHYSETERIDAE
GENUS: PHYSETER
SPECIES: P. MACROCEPHALUS

ORCA WHALE *Orcinus orca*

CONSERVATION STATUS: DATA DEFICIENT

Orcas, also called killer whales, are black with a white underside and white markings near their eyes. It is the largest member of the dolphin species and found in every ocean of the world. They are very social animals and live in family groups called pods.

BY THE NUMBERS		CLASSIFICATION
3–50	Pod size	**KINGDOM:** ANIMALIA
90 YEARS	Average female life expectancy in the wild	**PHYLUM:** CHORDATA **CLASS:** MAMMALIA **ORDER:** ARTIODACTYLA **INFRAORDER:** CETACEA **FAMILY:** DELPHINIDAE
60 YEARS	Average male life expectancy in the wild	**GENUS:** ORCINUS **SPECIES:** O. ORCA

KILLER WHALE KINGS

Orcas are also known for being at the top of the ocean's food chain because they have a wide range of prey, including smaller whales, dolphins, sea lions, turtles, otters, squid, octopus, and sea birds.

COMMON BOTTLENOSE DOLPHIN *Tursiops truncatus*

CONSERVATION STATUS: LEAST CONCERN

Bottlenose dolphins get their name from their thick, short snout that is similar to the shape of a bottle. Bottlenose dolphins are black to light gray in color, with white bellies and a stripe from their eye to the base of their flipper. These dolphins are very social and live in groups called pods. These pods can vary based on age, such as nursery pods of females and their offspring, pods of juveniles, and pods of adult males. Bottlenose dolphins have teeth, but they do not use them to chew food. Instead, they use their teeth to grip fish while they swallow them whole, headfirst, so the spines of the fish don't damage their throat.

BY THE NUMBERS	
22 MPH	Cruising speed underwater
15–30 FEET	Amount of food an adult bottlenose can eat daily
15	Typical pod size

CLASSIFICATION

- KINGDOM: Animalia
- PHYLUM: Chordata
- CLASS: Mammalia
- ORDER: Artiodactyla
- INFRAORDER: Cetacea
- FAMILY: Delphinidae
- GENUS: Tursiops
- SPECIES: T. truncatus

HARBOR PORPOISE *Phocoena phocoena*

CONSERVATION STATUS: LEAST CONCERN

Harbor porpoises have small, plump bodies and a triangular-shaped dorsal fin, and lack a noticeable beak. They are black or dark gray in color with a dark stripe that runs from their mouth or eye down to the flipper on both sides, the color fading to white on their underside. They commonly live in pairs or small groups. They are shy animals who avoid boats and rarely jump out of the water. When they come up for air, they roll from beak to tail by arching their back. This makes a loud audible puffing sound heard above water.

BY THE NUMBERS	
2–5	Typical pod size
25 SECONDS	How often they surface to breathe
5–5.5 FEET	Length

CLASSIFICATION

KINGDOM: Animalia
PHYLUM: Chordata
CLASS: Mammalia
ORDER: Artiodactyla
INFRAORDER: Cetacea
FAMILY: Phocoenidae
GENUS: Phocoena
SPECIES: P. phocoena

Hippopotamuses

The Hippopotamidae family is made up of two genera and species. Both have stomachs with three chambers, although they are not ruminating animals. They also both have distinct elongated and relatively large, rectangular-shaped skulls.

ESTIMATED NUMBER OF HIPPOPOTAMIDAE SPECIES: 2

DID YOU KNOW? Although Hippos may look like pigs and have a name that means "river horse," they are actually more closely related to whales.

COMMON HIPPOPOTAMUS
Hippopotamus amphibius

CONSERVATION STATUS: VULNERABLE

Hippopotami, often referred to as hippos for short, are extremely large, bulky, barrel-shaped animals. Their skin is very thin and purplish gray or slate gray in color, and brownish pink around their eyes and ears. Hippopotami live in groups of 20-100 members, with the females and their offspring in the middle of the resting pool and the males protecting them along the perimeter of the group. They lack sweat and scent glands and instead have mucous glands that secrete an oily red pigment that acts as a sunscreen agent and prevents the growth of bacteria on their skin.

BY THE NUMBERS		CLASSIFICATION
2,866–7,055 POUNDS	Weight	**KINGDOM:** Animalia **PHYLUM:** Chordata **CLASS:** Mammalia **ORDER:** Artiodactyla **FAMILY:** Hippopotamidae **GENUS:** Hippopotamus **SPECIES:** H. amphibius
150°	How far a hippo's jaws can open	
20 INCHES	Length of each canine tooth	

HIDING HIPPOS

Hippos are semi-aquatic animals, sleeping during the day in shallow water that is deep enough to submerge their bodies. Their eyes, ears, and nostrils are placed high on their head to remain above water and stay alert; but if completely submerged, the nostrils close and the ears fold to prevent water from entering them.

HIPPOPOTAMIDAE
Hippopotamuses

HIPPOPOTAMUS
True Hippopotamus

CHOEROPSIS
Pygmy Hippopotamus

PYGMY HIPPOPOTAMUS
Choeropsis liberiensis

CONSERVATION STATUS: ENDANGERED

Pygmy hippopotami have dark brown or gray skin on top, which fades to a lighter flesh color on their underside, and are significantly smaller in size than common hippopotomi. During the daytime, they rest in water to protect their skin from the sun or hide out along the riverbank and sleep. They sleep in the ground in small caves and burrows for a few days at a time, before finding a new location to call home.

SOLO HIPPO

Pygmy hippopotami are solitary animals and live alone except during mating times or when with their offspring. Pygmy hippopotami are nocturnal and are mostly active from late afternoon until midnight, which are their dedicated feeding hours.

BY THE NUMBERS	
353–606 POUNDS	Weight
100–150 POUNDS	Weight of grass a pygmy hippopotamus can consume daily
5–6 MINUTES	Length of time an adult can be underwater without air

CLASSIFICATION

- **KINGDOM:** Animalia
- **PHYLUM:** Chordata
- **CLASS:** Mammalia
- **ORDER:** Artiodactyla
- **FAMILY:** Hippopotamidae
- **SUBFAMILY:** Hippopotaminae
- **GENUS:** Choeropsis
- **SPECIES:** C. liberiensis

GIRAFFIDAE

Giraffe

The Giraffidae family consists of two living species, the giraffe and the okapi. Members of this family are ruminants and have long dark-colored tongues, lobed canine teeth, and ossicones, which are horns covered in skin.

ESTIMATED NUMBER OF GIRAFFIDAE SPECIES	2
DID YOU KNOW?	*While the Giraffidae are currently limited to Africa, their range once stretched across Eurasia.*

GIRAFFE NAP

Giraffes generally sleep while standing, although occasionally they will lay down.

GIRAFFIDAE
Giraffes and Okapi

GIRAFFA *Giraffes*

OKAPIA *Okapis*

GIRAFFE *Giraffa camelopardalis*

CONSERVATION STATUS: VULNERABLE

The giraffe is the tallest living animal in the world. It is easily identifiable by its long neck and white coat with a brown spotted pattern. It has a short, brown mane down the length of its back and a long tail with a black tuft of hair at the end. Giraffes' horns, called ossicones, are bones covered in skin and hair. Giraffes have a purplish-black prehensile tongue that grabs leaves from small branches.

BY THE NUMBERS

15 MINUTES	*Time from birth until a calf is able to stand*
2 FEET	*Average size of a giraffe's heart*
45°	*Distance a giraffe has to spread its legs apart in order to drink*

CLASSIFICATION

KINGDOM: Animalia
PHYLUM: Chordata
CLASS: Mammalia
ORDER: Artiodactyla
FAMILY: Giraffidae
GENUS: Giraffa
SPECIES: G. camelopardalis

URSIDAE

Bears

The Ursidae family is made of animals called bears. They are large with stocky legs, small eyes, round forward-facing ears, and short tails. Each paw has five curved claws that are non-retractable.

ESTIMATED NUMBER OF URSIDAE SPECIES: 8

DID YOU KNOW? *The word "bear" literally means "the brown one" and was likely a euphemism among ancient hunters eager to avoid an encounter with such a fearsome foe.*

URSIDAE
Bears

AILUROPODINAE
Giant Pandas

URSINAE

TREMARCTINAE
Spectacled Bears

HELARCTOS
Sun Bears

MELURSUS
Sloth Bears

URSUS

URSUS AMERICANUS
American Black Bears

URSUS THIBETANUS
Asiatic Black Bears

URSUS ARCTOS
Brown Bears

URSUS MARITIMUS
Polar Bears

POLAR BEAR *Ursus maritimus*

CONSERVATION STATUS: VULNERABLE

Polar bears are large and stocky. They have black skin with hollow, clear fur that lacks pigment. Their fur appears white due to light refraction (the bending of light). They have large, broad paws that are used for swimming in arctic waters. Each paw is covered in soft, small bumps called papillae, which provides traction as they walk on ice. Polar bears primarily eat the blubber of seals and leave the meat for other animals to feed on.

BY THE NUMBERS	
1–4	Cubs per litter
12 INCHES	Width of an adult paw
2 MINUTES	Average time polar bears can hold their breath while diving under water

CLASSIFICATION

KINGDOM: ANIMALIA
PHYLUM: CHORDATA
CLASS: MAMMALIA
ORDER: CARNIVORA
FAMILY: URSIDAE
GENUS: URSUS
SPECIES: U. MARITIMUS

GIANT PANDA *Ailuropoda melanoleuca*

CONSERVATION STATUS: VULNERABLE

Giant pandas are the rarest members of the bear family and are well known for their distinctive black-and-white pattern. Black markings cover their ears, eyes, shoulders, and limbs. They eat large portions of bamboo shoots and leaves daily with the help of their "thumbs." These "thumbs" are extensions of their wrist bone, which help them hold and grip bamboo stems like a thumb would. Giant pandas only digest about a fifth of what they consume, so they need to eat nearly 15% of their body weight each day to get the nutrients their bodies need.

BY THE NUMBERS	
3–5 OUNCES	*Weight at birth*
70 DAYS	*Average time until a cub can crawl*
12 HOURS	*Daily time spent eating*

CLASSIFICATION
KINGDOM: ANIMALIA
PHYLUM: CHORDATA
CLASS: MAMMALIA
ORDER: CARNIVORA
FAMILY: URSIDAE
GENUS: AILUROPODA
SPECIES: A. MELANOLEUCA

KODIAK BEAR *Ursus arctos middendorffi*

CONSERVATION STATUS: LEAST CONCERN

Kodiak bears are a subspecies of the brown bear and native to southwestern Alaska. They are very large and range in color from tan to orange to dark brown. Most Kodiak bears spend the winter hibernating in their den, although some males stay awake for the duration of the season. Females usually den the longest, from late October until late June, while males will emerge in early April.

BY THE NUMBERS	
3 YEARS	*Time cubs spend with their mother*
10 FEET	*Height of an adult male standing on his hind legs*
1,400 POUNDS	*Weight of an adult male*

CLASSIFICATION
KINGDOM: ANIMALIA
PHYLUM: CHORDATA
CLASS: MAMMALIA
ORDER: CARNIVORA
FAMILY: URSIDAE
GENUS: URSUS
SPECIES: U. ARCTOS
SUBSPECIES: U. A. MIDDENDORFFI

THE BEAR DIET

Kodiak bears are omnivores, eating salmon, berries, plants, and grasses.

GRIZZLY BEAR *Ursus arctos horribilis*

CONSERVATION STATUS: LEAST CONCERN

Grizzly bears are a subspecies of brown bear, located in parts of Canada and the United States. Although they are most often brown in color, they can range from black to blond and relying on color alone for identification can be misleading. Other unique factors include large muscle mass over their shoulders that looks similar to a hump, a concave-shaped face around the eyes, long claws for digging, and short, round ears. Grizzly bears are omnivores that eat a variety of foods based upon season and availability. They spend around five months during winter hibernating in dens of rock cavities or holes they dig in the ground. Grizzly bears are also one of the more aggressive bear species.

BY THE NUMBERS	
3–7 DAYS	*Time to create a den*
1 TON	*Average amount of material a grizzly bear moves when creating a den*
8–19 BEATS PER MINUTE	*Heart rate during hibernation*

CLASSIFICATION

KINGDOM: ANIMALIA
PHYLUM: CHORDATA
CLASS: MAMMALIA
ORDER: CARNIVORA
FAMILY: URSIDAE
GENUS: URSUS
SPECIES: U. ARCTOS
SUBSPECIES: U. A. HORRIBILIS

AMERICAN BLACK BEAR
Ursus americanus

CONSERVATION STATUS: LEAST CONCERN

Black bears commonly have a black coat, although sometimes they are cinnamon, brown, blond, gray, or white in color. They have brown muzzles and longer ears than other bears, and their face has a straight side profile. They have short, non-retractable claws that are used for climbing trees. Female black bears typically give birth every other year. With each pregnancy, they have a delayed implantation where the fertilized eggs float freely and are not implanted into the uterus until the female gains enough weight. Fetal development begins around the last half of the gestation (pregnancy) period.

BY THE NUMBERS		CLASSIFICATION
220 DAYS	Gestation (pregnancy) period	KINGDOM: ANIMALIA PHYLUM: CHORDATA CLASS: MAMMALIA ORDER: CARNIVORA FAMILY: URSIDAE GENUS: URSUS SPECIES: U. AMERICANUS
20–30%	Reduction of body weight after hibernation	
70%	Black bears in the United States with a black coat	

SLOTH BEAR *Melursus ursinus*

CONSERVATION STATUS: VULNERABLE

Sloth bears are unique members of the bear family and are unrelated to sloths. They have a shaggy coat that is either cinnamon, dark brown, or black in color with a distinct cream-colored patch on their chest shaped in a "U," "V," or "Y" pattern. Their diet consists primarily of fruit or termites. When hunting for termites, sloth bears dig in the earth using their curved front claws and break through hard termite nests. Then they use their long snouts to blow away the dirt and suck the termites up with their mouths like a vacuum. They lack front two teeth to aid in the process, and their nostrils can close on-demand to prevent dust and insects from entering.

BY THE NUMBERS		CLASSIFICATION
7 POUND	Birth weight	KINGDOM: ANIMALIA PHYLUM: CHORDATA CLASS: MAMMALIA ORDER: CARNIVORA FAMILY: URSIDAE SUBFAMILY: URSINAE GENUS: MELURSUS SPECIES: M. URSINUS
3 FEET	Distance they can detect termites underground	
100 POUNDS	Boulder weight they can move	

SUN BEAR *Helarctos malayanus*

CONSERVATION STATUS: VULNERABLE

Sun bears are the smallest of all the bear species. They are black with an orangish-colored muzzle and U-shaped patch on their chest. It is believed that they got their name from this patch, which some say looks like the rising or setting sun. They are excellent climbers and spend the majority of their life within tree canopies. They use their long tongues to get honey or insects from hard-to-reach places and feed on large amounts of fruit. Sun bears do not hibernate, probably because they live in tropical locations where there is plenty of food year round.

BY THE NUMBERS		CLASSIFICATION
10 INCHES	Length of tongue	KINGDOM: ANIMALIA
		PHYLUM: CHORDATA
		CLASS: MAMMALIA
60–143 POUNDS	Average weight	ORDER: CARNIVORA
		FAMILY: URSIDAE
		SUBFAMILY: URSINAE
30 MILES PER HOUR	Top speed	GENUS: HELARCTOS
		HORSFIELD, 1825
		SPECIES: H. MALAYANUS

EURASIAN BROWN BEAR
Ursus arctos arctos

CONSERVATION STATUS: LEAST CONCERN

Eurasian brown bears, also known as European brown bears, live within the mountain ranges of Europe and Asia. Male Eurasian brown bears are typically 10–20% larger in weight and length than females. They have a short tail that hides in a dense, long coat. They are omnivores, with the majority of their diet coming from fruit, seeds, roots, insects, fish, and other mammals. Eurasian brown bears are solitary animals and live alone except for times of mating or as cubs, staying with their mothers until approximately 2 years old.

BY THE NUMBERS		CLASSIFICATION
5 INCHES	Length of coat	KINGDOM: ANIMALIA
		PHYLUM: CHORDATA
		CLASS: MAMMALIA
15% MEAT	Diet	ORDER: CARNIVORA
		FAMILY: URSIDAE
		GENUS: URSUS
20,000 CALORIES PER DAY	Food intake in summer and fall months	SPECIES: U. ARCTOS
		SUBSPECIES: U. A. ARCTOS

LAGOMORPHA

Rabbits, Hares, and Pikas

The Lagomorpha order is made up of rabbits, hares, and pikas. Although they may look similar to rodents in the Rodentia order, the distinguishing difference between the two orders is the extra set of short, peg-like incisor teeth that members of Lagomorpha have behind their long, continuously growing incisors.

ESTIMATED NUMBER OF LAGOMORPHA SPECIES: 109

DID YOU KNOW? *All Lagomorpha once looked like Pikas. It took thousands of years of evolution to develop the characteristic hind legs of rabbits and hares.*

LAGOMORPHA
Rabbits, Hares, and Pikas

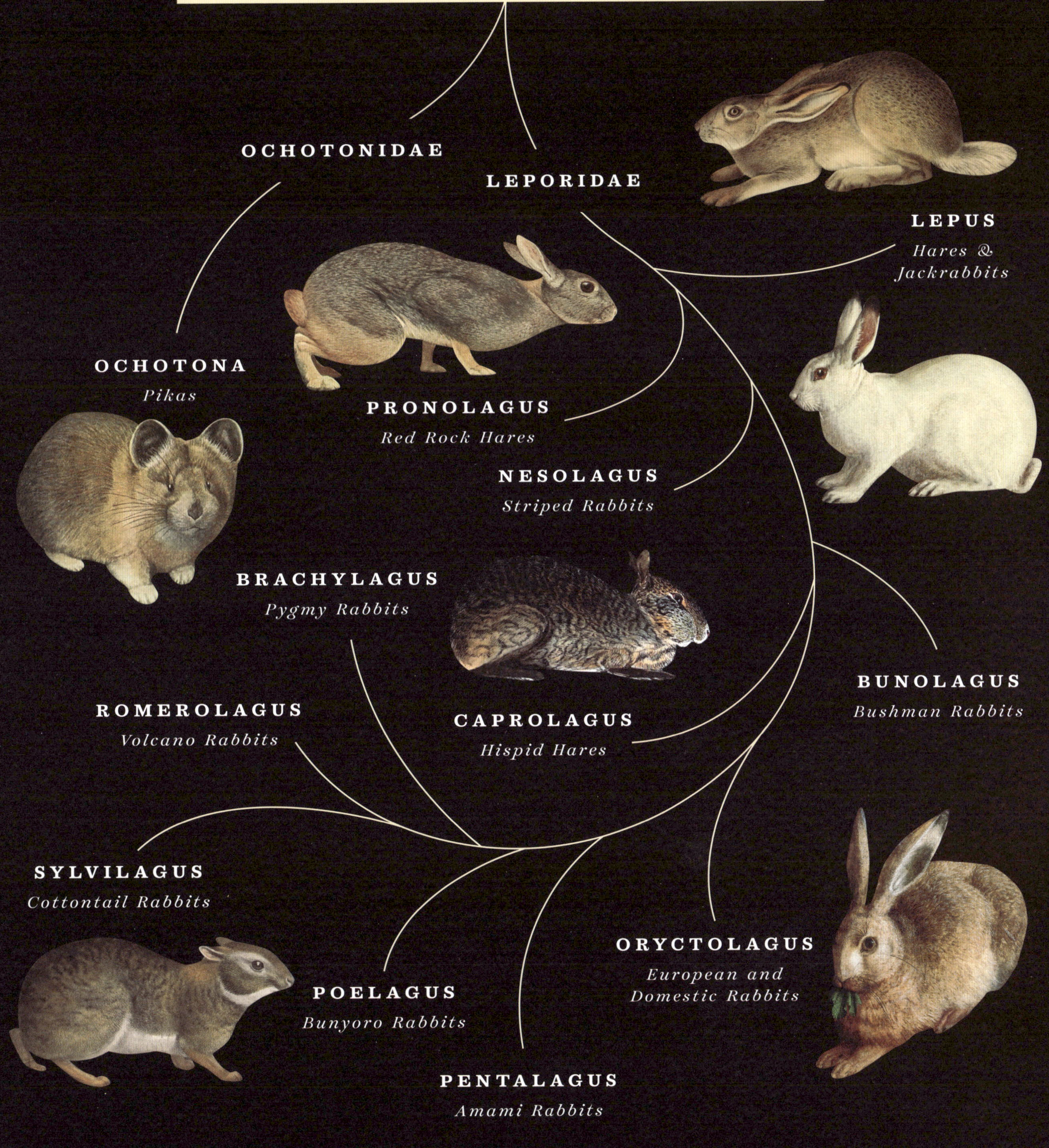

OCHOTONIDAE

LEPORIDAE

LEPUS
Hares & Jackrabbits

OCHOTONA
Pikas

PRONOLAGUS
Red Rock Hares

NESOLAGUS
Striped Rabbits

BRACHYLAGUS
Pygmy Rabbits

BUNOLAGUS
Bushman Rabbits

ROMEROLAGUS
Volcano Rabbits

CAPROLAGUS
Hispid Hares

SYLVILAGUS
Cottontail Rabbits

ORYCTOLAGUS
European and Domestic Rabbits

POELAGUS
Bunyoro Rabbits

PENTALAGUS
Amami Rabbits

CAPE HARE *Lepus capensis*

CONSERVATION STATUS: LEAST CONCERN

Cape hares, also commonly called desert hares, are found in parts of Africa, the Middle East, and Central Asia. They are identified by the white outline around their eyes and long, upright ears. They live in hot, dry deserts or agricultural areas. They are known for their athletic abilities as fast runners and good swimmers and climbers. They have excellent vision, which helps protect against predators.

BY THE NUMBERS

360°	Direction they can see
48 MILES PER HOUR	Top speed
1 MINUTE	Average amount of deep sleep per day

CLASSIFICATION

KINGDOM: ANIMALIA
PHYLUM: CHORDATA
CLASS: MAMMALIA
ORDER: LAGOMORPHA
FAMILY: LEPORIDAE
GENUS: LEPUS
SPECIES: L. CAPENSIS

WOOLLY HARE *Lepus oiostolus*

CONSERVATION STATUS: LEAST CONCERN

Woolly hares live in grassland habitats in parts of China, Nepal, and India. The females are larger in size than the males, but they both have the same tail and hind leg lengths. Their coats molt, or shed, once a year. They are herbivores that most commonly eat grasses and young leaves. Woolly hares usually live and rest in dens, which hide them from predators.

BY THE NUMBERS	
2	Litters per year
4–6	Leverets (babies) per litter
5.3 POUNDS	Average female weight

CLASSIFICATION

KINGDOM: ANIMALIA
PHYLUM: CHORDATA
CLASS: MAMMALIA
ORDER: LAGOMORPHA
FAMILY: LEPORIDAE
GENUS: LEPUS
SPECIES: L. OIOSTOLUS

DOMESTICATED RABBIT *Oryctolagus cuniculus domesticus*

CONSERVATION STATUS: NOT EVALUATED

Domesticated rabbits are believed to have originated from European descent in the 1500s. Today they are known for being a global pet. They are crepuscular animals, which means they are most active at dawn and dusk. Domesticated rabbits need a diet of primarily hay, fresh vegetables, and limited amounts of pellets.

BY THE NUMBERS	
10–12 YEARS	*Lifespan*
80	*Recognized breeds*
3RD PLACE	*Ranking of America's most popular pets*

CLASSIFICATION

- KINGDOM: Animalia
- PHYLUM: Chordata
- CLASS: Mammalia
- ORDER: Lagomorpha
- FAMILY: Leporidae
- GENUS: Oryctolagus
- SPECIES: O. cuniculus
- SUBSPECIES: O. C. subsp. domesticus

BUNNY BUDDIES

Domestic rabbits are social creatures that prefer companionship.

BUNNY BEDTIME

European rabbits are nocturnal and stay in their warrens during the daytime and forage above ground for food at night.

EUROPEAN RABBIT *Oryctolagus cuniculus*

CONSERVATION STATUS: ENDANGERED

European rabbits were found in the Iberian peninsula and parts of France and Africa after the last ice age. Due to human movement and the rabbit's ability to adapt, the European rabbit is now found worldwide, with the exception of Asia and Antarctica. European rabbits live in groups called colonies that consist of both males and females. These colonies live underground in complex burrows called warrens. Each colony is a male-dominated hierarchy that determines mating privileges.

BY THE NUMBERS	
6–10	Colony size
8 MONTHS	Age of maturity
9 YEARS	Lifespan

CLASSIFICATION

KINGDOM: ANIMALIA
PHYLUM: CHORDATA
CLASS: MAMMALIA
ORDER: LAGOMORPHA
FAMILY: LEPORIDAE
GENUS: ORYCTOLAGUS
SPECIES: O. CUNICULUS

COMMON TAPETI *Sylvilagus brasiliensis*

CONSERVATION STATUS: ENDANGERED

Common tapetis, also known as Brazilian cottontails, live in areas ranging from southern Mexico to northern Argentina, including Ecuador, Amazonian Peru, Bolivia, Brazil, and Paraguay. They live in damp rain forested areas, as well as forests and grasslands. Common tapetis don't live in underground burrows, but pregnant females will dig small depressions in the earth for their nests that they then line with grasses and fur. They huddle over the nest to feed their kits (babies) once they are born. Kits are born with their eyes open and are ready to leave the nest once they are weaned.

BY THE NUMBERS	
26–30 DAYS	Gestation (pregnancy) period
2	Average number of kits (babies)
14–18 DAYS	Age kits are weaned

CLASSIFICATION

- KINGDOM: Animalia
- PHYLUM: Chordata
- CLASS: Mammalia
- ORDER: Lagomorpha
- FAMILY: Leporidae
- GENUS: Sylvilagus
- SPECIES: S. brasiliensis

ARCTIC ADAPTATIONS

Unlike desert hares, arctic hares have shorter ears that they can warm up more efficiently. They also have sharp claws that can dig through snow and ice to get food.

ARCTIC HARE *Lepus arcticus*

CONSERVATION STATUS: LEAST CONCERN

Arctic hares are brown and gray during summer months and molt (shed) their fur by winter, which grows back in white with black-tipped ears. This helps them blend in with the snowy winter landscape, making it more difficult for predators to spot them. They have strong hind legs that they stand up on to listen for potential dangers. They can jump from this upright position and will use this tactic if threatened by a predator.

BY THE NUMBERS	
2 FEET	Average length
40 MILES PER HOUR	Top speed
6.8 FEET	Length of their jump

CLASSIFICATION

KINGDOM: ANIMALIA
PHYLUM: CHORDATA
CLASS: MAMMALIA
ORDER: LAGOMORPHA
FAMILY: LEPORIDAE
GENUS: LEPUS
SPECIES: L. ARCTICUS

XENARTHRA

Anteaters, Sloths, and Armadillos

The biological Xenarthra superorder is made up of sloths, armadillos, and anteaters. All animals in this superorder have extra joints in their lower spine and are placental animals. A placental mammal, similar to a human, is nourished within the mother's womb by an organ called the placenta, and is born well-developed.

| ESTIMATED NUMBER OF XENARTHRA SPECIES | 31 |

DID YOU KNOW? *Xenarthra are named for their flexible spines and extra joints. The word is Greek for "strange joints."*

XENARTHRA
Anteaters, Sloths, and Armadillos

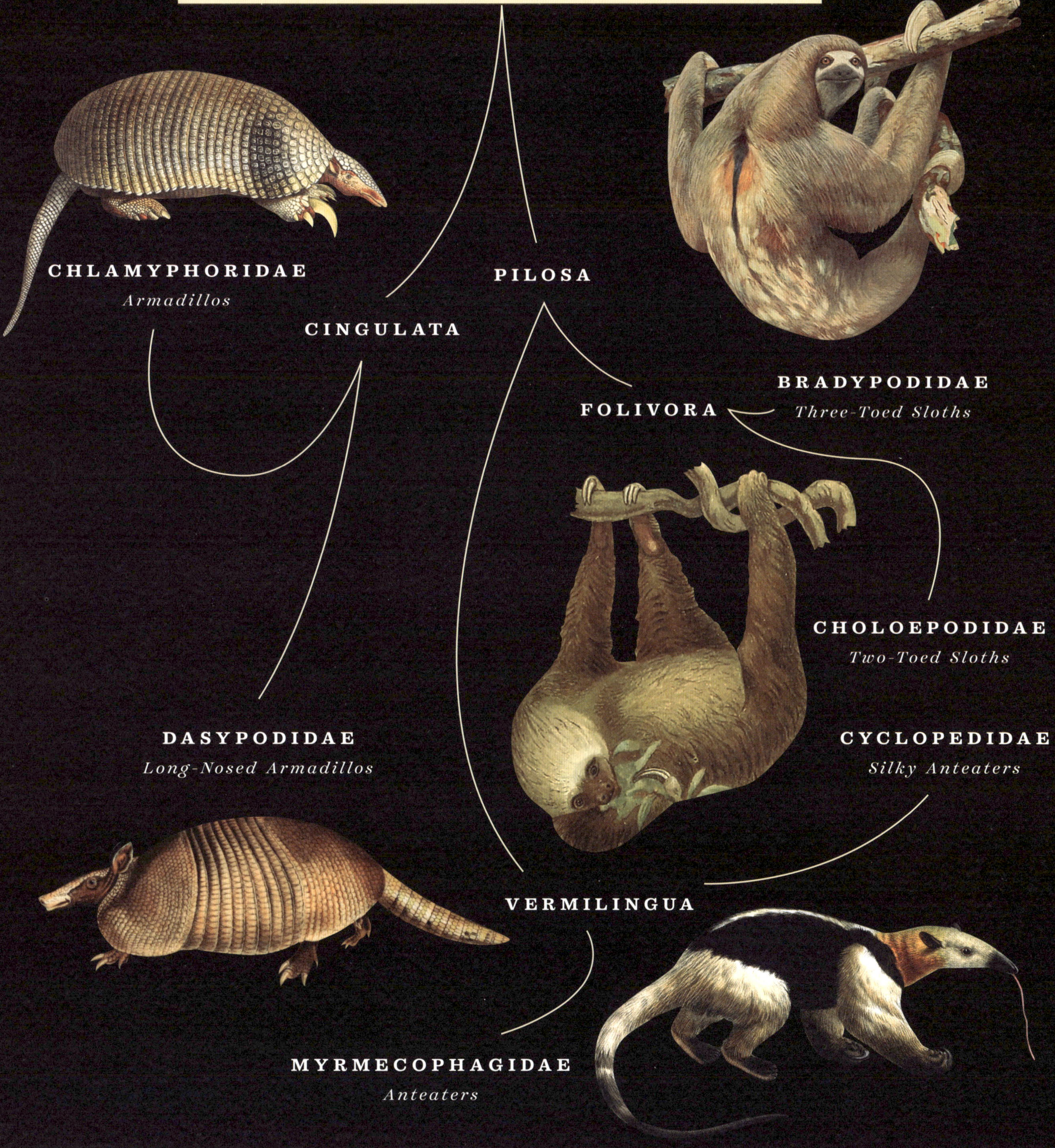

CHLAMYPHORIDAE
Armadillos

PILOSA

CINGULATA

BRADYPODIDAE
Three-Toed Sloths

FOLIVORA

CHOLOEPODIDAE
Two-Toed Sloths

CYCLOPEDIDAE
Silky Anteaters

DASYPODIDAE
Long-Nosed Armadillos

VERMILINGUA

MYRMECOPHAGIDAE
Anteaters

NINE-BANDED ARMADILLO *Dasypus novemcinctus*

CONSERVATION STATUS: LEAST CONCERN

Nine-banded armadillos live in South, Central, and North America. They have a thick armored shell that consists of bony plates covered in a leathery-type skin. The area of their shell along the back has bands that allow them to bend and gives nine-banded armadillos their name and identifying feature. They have strong claws for digging burrows, which are used for sleeping, nesting sites, food traps, and places of warmth during the cold. Nine-banded armadillos generally feed on insects like ants, termites, and worms. They loosen the dirt with their long nose and use their sticky tongue to grab them.

BY THE NUMBERS	
16% OF BODY WEIGHT	Armored shell
6 MINUTES	Length of time they can hold their breath under water
8 INCHES	Depth their nose is able to detect insects belowground

CLASSIFICATION	
KINGDOM:	Animalia
PHYLUM:	Chordata
CLASS:	Mammalia
ORDER:	Cingulata
FAMILY:	Dasypodidae
GENUS:	Dasypus
SPECIES:	D. novemcinctus

GIANT ARMADILLO *Priodontes maximus*

CONSERVATION STATUS: VULNERABLE

Giant armadillos are the largest living species of armadillo. They live in the tropical forests and grasslands of South America. Giant armadillos have three claws on their forefeet, with the middle claw being very long and curved downward. This long claw allows them to efficiently dig burrows in the ground where they sleep during the daytime. Giant armadillos are able to stand on their hind legs, using their tail for balance. This technique allows them to reach into high termite mounds at mealtime and scare off potential predators by appearing more threatening.

BY THE NUMBERS	
5 FEET	Length including tail
41–72 POUNDS	Weight
80–100	Teeth

CLASSIFICATION

- KINGDOM: Animalia
- PHYLUM: Chordata
- CLASS: Mammalia
- ORDER: Cingulata
- FAMILY: Chlamyphoridae
- SUBFAMILY: Tolypeutinae
- GENUS: Priodontes
- SPECIES: P. maximus

GIANT ANTEATER *Myrmecophaga tridactyla*

CONSERVATION STATUS: VULNERABLE

Giant anteaters live in Central and South America in wetlands, grasslands, and tropical forests. They are the largest anteater species, with a distinct bushy tail and long snout. They have black stripes that circle their body from their chest toward their spine. Giant anteaters can tear open termite and ant nests using their strong front feet and claws. They repeatedly flick their long tongue into the nest, which is coated in a layer of sticky saliva. This saliva helps the insects adhere to the tongue as it moves into the anteater's mouth, where they will be eaten.

BY THE NUMBERS

30,000	*Daily intake of ants and termites*
2 FEET	*Length of tongue*
150 TIMES PER MINUTE	*Tongue flicks in and out*

CLASSIFICATION

- **KINGDOM:** ANIMALIA
- **PHYLUM:** CHORDATA
- **CLASS:** MAMMALIA
- **ORDER:** PILOSA
- **FAMILY:** MYRMECOPHAGIDAE
- **GENUS:** MYRMECOPHAGA
- **SPECIES:** M. TRIDACTYLA

SOUTHERN TAMANDUA *Tamandua tetradactyla*

CONSERVATION STATUS: LEAST CONCERN

Southern tamanduas are both arboreal and terrestrial, meaning they live both in trees and on the ground. They have a hairless prehensile tail used to help grip tree branches as it moves throughout the canopy. They have four sharp, curved claws on their front feet and five on their hind feet. To keep from puncturing their palms, southern tamanduas walk on the outside of their feet at an angle. If threatened by a predator, they may hiss or release a foul-smelling odor from their anal gland. If that doesn't work, they will brace themselves on their hind legs, using their tail for extra balance, and will grab or attack their opponent with their powerful forearms and claws.

BY THE NUMBERS	
0.25 INCHES	Mouth opening
91°F	Body temperature
4X STRONGER	The southern tamandua's odor compared to a skunk's

CLASSIFICATION	
KINGDOM:	Animalia
PHYLUM:	Chordata
CLASS:	Mammalia
ORDER:	Pilosa
FAMILY:	Myrmecophagidae
GENUS:	Tamandua
SPECIES:	T. tetradactyla

SLOW LIVING

The two-toed sloth's coat can turn a greenish tint due to algae growth and is home to ticks, moths, and beetles.

LINNAEUS'S TWO-TOED SLOTH *Choloepus didactylus*

CONSERVATION STATUS: LEAST CONCERN

Two-toed sloths are known for being one of the slowest mammals on earth. This is because they have a very slow metabolism and need to conserve energy. They primarily eat leaves that can stay in their digestive tract for up to one month. They spend most of their life hanging upside down from tree branches and only come down to defecate (go to the bathroom) or to change trees for new food sources. They have a unique coat that grows upward, from their stomach to their back, that helps water run off during rainstorms. Like their name, Linnaeus's two-toed sloths have two toes and claws on their front feet that are between 3–4 inches long, while their hind feet have three toes and claws.

BY THE NUMBERS	
1 TIME PER WEEK	Defecate
74–92°F	Body temperature range
15 HOURS	Daily sleep

CLASSIFICATION
KINGDOM: ANIMALIA
PHYLUM: CHORDATA
CLASS: MAMMALIA
ORDER: PILOSA
FAMILY: CHOLOEPODIDAE
GENUS: CHOLOEPUS
SPECIES: C. DIDACTYLUS

MANED SLOTH *Bradypus torquatus*

CONSERVATION STATUS: VULNERABLE

Maned sloths live in the Brazilian Atlantic rainforests. They are identifiable by the three toes on each foot and the lack of markings on their face. Males have black on the dorsal, or top area, of their mane that distinguishes them from females. Most mammals have seven vertebrae, but maned sloths have eight or nine that allow them to rotate their head further. They have very little muscle mass, allowing them to hang on thin branches. They spend most of their time camouflaged in tree canopies because they cannot stand or walk on the ground. If they must come down, they drag their body along the ground using their front legs and claws.

BY THE NUMBERS	
270°	Head rotation
5.9 INCHES	Mane length
6–9 MONTHS	Cubs cling to their mother

CLASSIFICATION

- **KINGDOM:** ANIMALIA
- **PHYLUM:** CHORDATA
- **CLASS:** MAMMALIA
- **ORDER:** PILOSA
- **FAMILY:** BRADYPODIDAE
- **GENUS:** BRADYPUS
- **SPECIES:** B. TORQUATUS

EULIPOTYPHLA

Hedgehogs, Moles, and Shrews

The Eulipotyphla order is made up of shrews, moles, gymnures, hedgehogs, and solenodons. Animals in this order have long, pointed snouts, small ears, many sharp teeth, and small eyes that, in some species, are almost non-functioning.

ESTIMATED NUMBER OF EULIPOTYPHLA SPECIES | **450**

DID YOU KNOW? "Eulipotyphla" means "truly fat and blind," which seems a little unfair to some of these mammals.

EULIPOTYPHLA
Hedgehogs, Moles, and Shrews

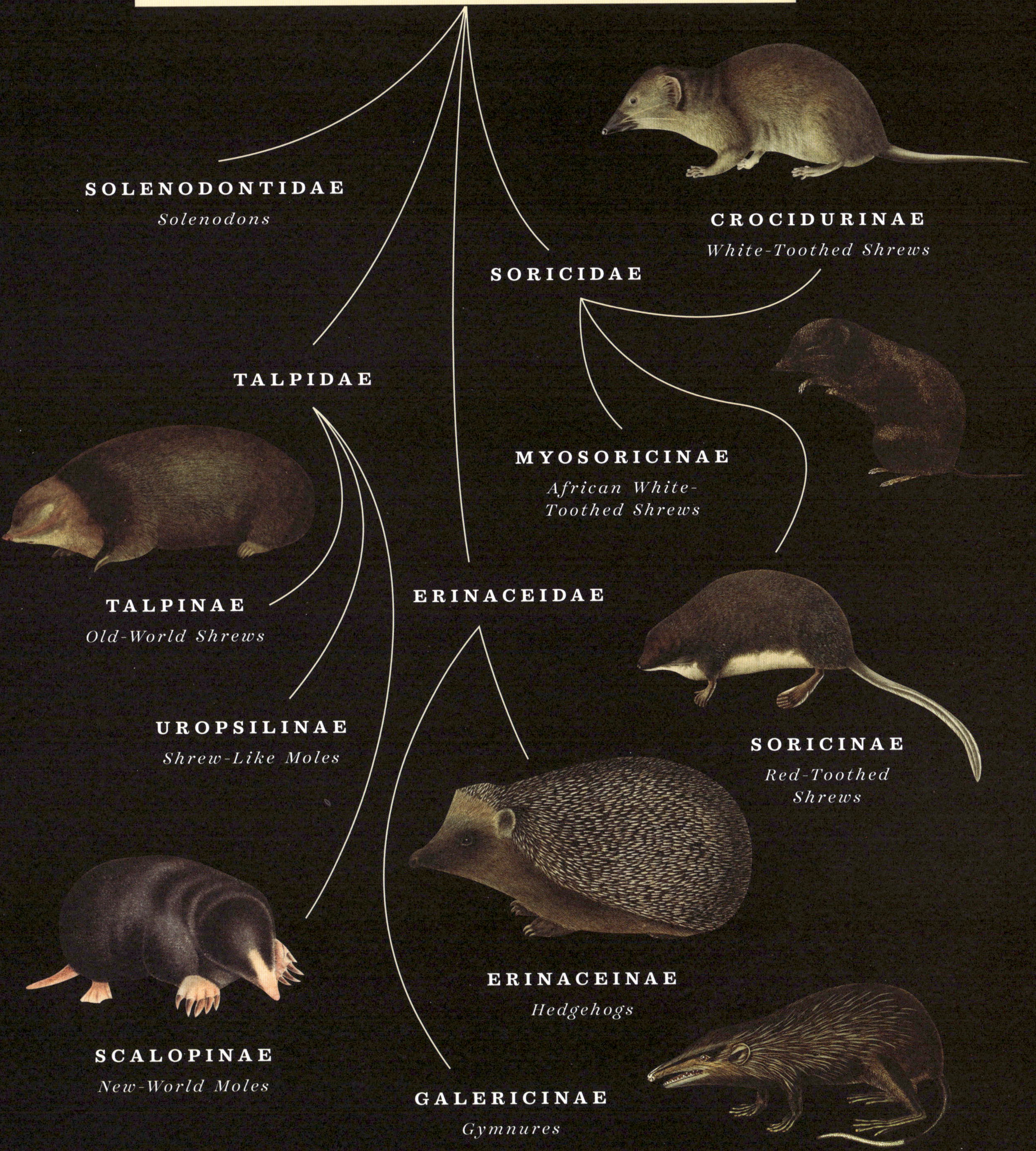

SOLENODONTIDAE
Solenodons

TALPIDAE

TALPINAE
Old-World Shrews

UROPSILINAE
Shrew-Like Moles

SCALOPINAE
New-World Moles

SORICIDAE

CROCIDURINAE
White-Toothed Shrews

MYOSORICINAE
African White-Toothed Shrews

SORICINAE
Red-Toothed Shrews

ERINACEIDAE

ERINACEINAE
Hedgehogs

GALERICINAE
Gymnures

EUROPEAN HEDGEHOG *Erinaceus europaeus*

CONSERVATION STATUS: LEAST CONCERN	BY THE NUMBERS		CLASSIFICATION
European hedgehogs are small, round animals that live in fields and hedgerows throughout Europe and central Asia. European hedgehogs have coarse, yellowish-brown hair covering their cheeks, throat, stomach, and legs. The remainder of their body is covered in spines that are white at the base and tip and black and brown in the middle.	**5,000**	Approximate number of spines	KINGDOM: ANIMALIA PHYLUM: CHORDATA CLASS: MAMMALIA ORDER: EULIPOTYPHLA FAMILY: ERINACEIDAE GENUS: ERINACEUS SPECIES: E. EUROPAEUS
	¾–1 INCH	Length of spines	
	6 YEARS	Lifespan	

HEDGEHOG HAIR

Each spine is hollow and made of keratin. Each spine grows from a follicle, similar to human hair, that is attached to a thin layer of muscle. This sheet of muscle allows their spines to become erect all together at once while rolled into a ball.

LONG-EARED HEDGEHOG *Hemiechinus auritus*

CONSERVATION STATUS: LEAST CONCERN

Long-eared hedgehogs are nocturnal animals with excellent hearing and smelling abilities. Most often they live in burrows that they dig for themselves beneath bushes, but occasionally they will overtake the vacant burrow of another animal. They forage for food at night, looking for grasshoppers, beetles, and other insects to eat. Long-eared hedgehogs breed once a year, between July and September. They give birth to hoglets (babies) that are naked, with only a few soft spines. Within five hours of birth, the spines quadruple in length. Two weeks after birth, the babies are fully covered in their tough spines.

BY THE NUMBERS	
18 INCHES	*Burrow length*
39 DAYS	*Gestation (pregnancy) period*
2–3	*Hoglets per litter*

CLASSIFICATION
KINGDOM: ANIMALIA
PHYLUM: CHORDATA
CLASS: MAMMALIA
ORDER: EULIPOTYPHLA
FAMILY: ERINACEIDAE
GENUS: HEMIECHINUS
SPECIES: H. AURITUS

STAR-NOSED MOLE *Condylura crista*

CONSERVATION STATUS: LEAST CONCERN

Star-nosed moles are a semi-aquatic animal from parts of North America. They live in the moist soil found in forests, marshes, meadows, and other areas near water. They have a unique nose, which consists of a symmetrically shaped star with tentacles on all sides. Each tentacle is covered in tiny papillae, called Eimer's organs. Eimer's organs act as receptors for identifying objects by feeling their texture. Because of this unique nose, star-nosed moles have the best sense of touch of any mammal.

BY THE NUMBERS	
22	Total number of tentacles
25,000	Total number of Eimer's organs/touch receptors
12 OBJECTS PER SECOND	Rate at which the tentacles can move

CLASSIFICATION

- **KINGDOM:** Animalia
- **PHYLUM:** Chordata
- **CLASS:** Mammalia
- **ORDER:** Eulipotyphla
- **FAMILY:** Talpidae
- **GENUS:** Condylura
- **SPECIES:** C. cristata

TOWNSEND'S MOLE *Scapanus townsendii*

CONSERVATION STATUS: LEAST CONCERN	BY THE NUMBERS		CLASSIFICATION
Townsend's moles live in the Pacific Northwest region of the United States and British Columbia, Canada. They have dark gray or black fur, a long pointed nose, small eyes, and no visible ears. They have very large front paws and claws, which are used for digging their burrows. Their diet consists of mostly earthworms, small invertebrates, and some plant material that they eat within their burrows.	70%	Percent of earthworms in their diet	KINGDOM: ANIMALIA PHYLUM: CHORDATA CLASS: MAMMALIA ORDER: EULIPOTYPHLA FAMILY: TALPIDAE GENUS: SCAPANUS SPECIES: S. TOWNSENDII
	44	Total number of teeth	
	5.9–7.9 INCHES	Burrowing depth	

AMERICAN WATER SHREW *Sorex palustris*

CONSERVATION STATUS: LEAST CONCERN

American water shrews are found throughout the northern parts of the United States, Alaska, and Canada. They are semi-aquatic and the smallest diving mammal. They dive into the water to forage for food as their diet consists of aquatic insects. Their hind feet are ideal for diving because they are large, webbed, and covered in bristlelike hair.

BY THE NUMBERS	
0.38–0.63 OUNCES	*Weight*
18 MONTHS	*Lifespan*
31.1–47.7 SECONDS	*Duration of dive*

CLASSIFICATION	
KINGDOM:	Animalia
PHYLUM:	Chordata
CLASS:	Mammalia
ORDER:	Eulipotyphla
FAMILY:	Soricidae
GENUS:	Sorex
SPECIES:	S. palustris

WATER WALKERS

American water shrews can even run across water for short periods of time as air bubbles get trapped in their fur and hair, allowing the surface tension of the water to support their weight.

EURASIAN SHREW *Sorex araneus*

CONSERVATION STATUS: LEAST CONCERN

Eurasian shrews, also known as common shrews, live throughout Eastern Europe, Scandinavia, and Great Britain. They are most easily identified by their red-tipped teeth and long, thick tails. They have a tri-colored fur coat that is dark brown along their back, light brown on their side, and white on their underside. They are solitary creatures and live alone except during mating season. Females may give birth to multiple litters a year, typically during May to September.

BY THE NUMBERS	
700 BEATS PER MINUTE	*Heart rate*
3–4	*Litters per year*
5–7	*Shrewlets (babies) per litter*

CLASSIFICATION

KINGDOM: ANIMALIA
PHYLUM: CHORDATA
CLASS: MAMMALIA
ORDER: EULIPOTYPHLA
FAMILY: SORICIDAE
GENUS: SOREX
SPECIES: S. ARANEUS

Rhinoceroses

The Rhinocerotidae family consists of five species. Members have very large bodies, an elongated skull, one to two horns, and very thick folded skin that gives the appearance of plated armor.

ESTIMATED NUMBER OF RHINOCEROTIDAE SPECIES	5

DID YOU KNOW? *Only five species of rhino exist today, but the extinct rhinoceros* Paraceratherium *was the largest land mammal ever.*

INDIAN RHINOCEROS
Rhinoceros unicornis

CONSERVATION STATUS: VULNERABLE

Indian rhinoceroses live in parts of Pakistan, India, Nepal, Bangladesh, and Assam in alluvial grassland, adjacent swamp, and wooded jungle habitats. Indian rhinoceroses are the largest of the three Asian rhinoceros species. They are identifiable by the single horn on their nose and their many skin folds, which give the appearance of armor. They are not as social as other species, nor do they maintain strong territories.

BY THE NUMBERS		CLASSIFICATION
30 MILES PER HOUR	*Top speed*	**KINGDOM:** ANIMALIA
		PHYLUM: CHORDATA
		CLASS: MAMMALIA
479 DAYS	*Gestation (pregnancy) period*	**ORDER:** PERISSODACTYLA
		FAMILY: RHINOCEROTIDAE
		GENUS: RHINOCEROS
40 YEARS	*Lifespan*	**SPECIES:** R. UNICORNIS

RHINO REPAST

Indian rhinoceroses eat a variety of grasses, leaves, fruits, branches, and other aquatic and cultivated plants. When eating aquatic plants, they will put their head completely underwater and pull the plant up by the roots using their mouth.

RHINOCEROTIDAE
Rhinoceroses

DICEROS BICORNIS	**CERATOTHERIUM SIMUM**	**RHINOCEROS UNICORNIS**	**RHINOCEROS SONDAICUS**	**DICERORHINUS SUMATRENSIS**
Black Rhinoceroses	*White Rhinoceroses*	*Indian Rhinoceroses*	*Javan Rhinoceroses*	*Sumatran Rhinoceroses*

WHITE RHINOCEROS *Ceratotherium simum*

CONSERVATION STATUS: NEAR THREATENED

White rhinoceroses, also called square-lipped rhinoceroses due to the flat shape of their mouth, live in Central and Southern Africa in long- and short-grass savannas. They are fairly social animals that live in small groups. The dominant male will protect his territory by marking the area with urine, feces, and foot stomping and damaging plants with his horn. They are generally peaceful animals but will use their horns to fight if needed.

BY THE NUMBERS

37–79 INCHES	Length of larger horn
4,000–6,000 POUNDS	Weight
5–6 FEET	Shoulder height

CLASSIFICATION

KINGDOM: ANIMALIA
PHYLUM: CHORDATA
CLASS: MAMMALIA
ORDER: PERISSODACTYLA
FAMILY: RHINOCEROTIDAE
GENUS: CERATOTHERIUM
SPECIES: C. SIMUM

MUSTELIDAE

Badgers, Weasels, and Otters

The Mustelidae family is made up of fifty-six species, including badgers, weasels, and otters. In general, members of the Mustelidae family have long bodies, short legs, a strong, thick neck, and a small head.

ESTIMATED NUMBER OF MUSTELIDAE SPECIES | **70**

DID YOU KNOW? *All mustelids but the sea otter have strong-smelling scent glands used to mark territory.*

MUSTELIDAE
Badgers, Weasels and Otters

MELLIVORINAE
Honey Badgers

HELICTIDINAE
Ferret-Badgers

GULONINAE
Martens

ICTONYCHINAE
Grisons & Polecats

LUTRINAE
Otters

TAXIDIINAE
American Badgers

MELES
European Badgers, Asian Badgers, Japanese Badgers & Caucasian Badgers

MELINAE

ARCTONYX
Hog Badgers

MUSTELINAE
Weasels, Ferrets & Minks

GREATER HOG BADGER *Arctonyx collaris*

CONSERVATION STATUS: VULNERABLE

Greater hog badgers are similar in appearance to European badgers; however, there are a few distinguishing characteristics, including larger white front claws and long white hairs along their tails. Greater hog badgers are omnivores, eating a mixture of earthworms, fruits, roots, and small animals. They locate their food using their snout, which is similar to a pig's. They also use their snouts, along with their incisors and lower canine teeth, to dig in the dirt to locate food, build burrows, or hide from approaching predators.

BY THE NUMBERS	
15–31 POUNDS	*Body weight*
33.5–52 INCHES	*Body and tail length*
2–4	*Cubs per litter*

CLASSIFICATION	
KINGDOM:	ANIMALIA
PHYLUM:	CHORDATA
CLASS:	MAMMALIA
ORDER:	CARNIVORA
FAMILY:	MUSTELIDAE
GENUS:	ARCTONYX
SPECIES:	A. COLLARIS

A WELL KEPT SETT

Badger setts remain very clean as European badgers do not bring food into them or defecate in them. Instead, they share communal toilets, small holes in the earth located on the edge of their territory away from the sett.

EUROPEAN BADGER *Meles meles*

CONSERVATION STATUS: LEAST CONCERN

European badgers are also commonly referred to as Eurasian badgers as they live throughout most of Europe and western Asia. They are nocturnal animals, which means that they are most active around sunrise and sunset. European badgers live in family groups called clans. They construct setts, which are underground burrow systems within the center of their clan's territory.

BY THE NUMBERS	
12 MEMBERS	Maximum clan size
115–266 FEET	Passage length of sett
5.5–12.6 INCHES	Passage height of setts

CLASSIFICATION	
KINGDOM:	ANIMALIA
PHYLUM:	CHORDATA
CLASS:	MAMMALIA
ORDER:	CARNIVORA
FAMILY:	MUSTELIDAE
GENUS:	MELES
SPECIES:	M. MELES

LEAST WEASEL *Mustela nivalis*

CONSERVATION STATUS: LEAST CONCERN

Least weasels are also referred to as common weasels. In certain regions, their color can change to white during the winter while remaining chocolate brown with a white underside the rest of the year. Least weasels must eat food regularly or else they will starve to death. It is common for them to kill prey larger than themselves, eat some of it, and store away the remainder for future meals. This behavior is known as caching. Least weasels conceal their caches near the entrance of their den or at their latrine (bathroom) site. These locations are then covered in their foul-smelling scent to ward off others from stealing their cache.

BY THE NUMBERS	
50% OF BODY WEIGHT	*Daily food consumption*
1–2 YEARS	*Lifespan*
34	*Teeth per weasel*

CLASSIFICATION
KINGDOM: ANIMALIA
PHYLUM: CHORDATA
CLASS: MAMMALIA
ORDER: CARNIVORA
FAMILY: MUSTELIDAE
GENUS: MUSTELA
SPECIES: M. NIVALIS

NORTH AMERICAN RIVER OTTER *Lontra canadensis*

CONSERVATION STATUS: LEAST CONCERN

North American river otters are sometimes referred to as Canadian otters because they live throughout Canada, Alaska, and parts of the United States. They live in both marine and freshwater areas, including rivers, lakes, streams, ponds, marshes, estuaries, and swamps. They are semi-aquatic animals that have webbed feet and dense layers of fur that repel water and help insulate their body from cold temperatures. They have long, sensitive whiskers that are used for hunting food underwater, as their sense of smell, sight, and hearing is greatly reduced. North American river otters live in dens made under logs, rocks, or from burrows of other animals. Females give birth in these dens, where their pups (babies) will stay until they begin to eat solid food.

BY THE NUMBERS	
850,000	*Hair per square inch*
8 MINUTES	*Time spent underwater without air*
2 MONTHS	*Pups emerge from den*

CLASSIFICATION
KINGDOM: ANIMALIA
PHYLUM: CHORDATA
CLASS: MAMMALIA
ORDER: CARNIVORA
FAMILY: MUSTELIDAE
GENUS: LONTRA
SPECIES: L. CANADENSIS

AMERICAN MINK *Neovison vison*

CONSERVATION STATUS: LEAST CONCERN

American minks are semi-aquatic with long, slender bodies and partially webbed feet. Their fur is dark brown in color with white patches on their chin and throat and contains an oily substance that helps repel water. They live in forested areas near water where they can build or take over another animal's burrow. American minks are very territorial of their home space and mark their areas with a foul-smelling scent. They fight other males who attempt to enter and spray unwanted intruders, similar to skunks. When content, they purr like cats.

BY THE NUMBERS	
100 FEET	*Swimming distance*
16.5 FEET	*Diving depth*
0.62–3.73 MILES	*Range of territory*

CLASSIFICATION	
KINGDOM:	Animalia
PHYLUM:	Chordata
CLASS:	Mammalia
ORDER:	Carnivora
FAMILY:	Mustelidae
GENUS:	Neogale
SPECIES:	N. vison

WARM WOLVERINES

Wolverines manage to live in cold climates because their fur is hydrophobic, or resistant to frost and snow.

WOLVERINE *Gulo gulo*

CONSERVATION STATUS: LEAST CONCERN

Wolverines are the largest land-dwelling member of the Mustelidae family. They have sharp claws that are semi-retractable and a very strong bite, which is known to crush bones. Wolverines live in cold, remote climates, largely becuase their diet consists of scavenging the meat of larger animals and storing it for later use. The cold climate helps preserve the meat and make it last longer. They mark their territory and food storage sites with scent gland secretions.

BY THE NUMBERS	
9.3 MILES PER HOUR	*Top running speed*
8.7 MILES	*Distance traveled daily*
40 POUNDS	*Weight*

CLASSIFICATION	
KINGDOM:	ANIMALIA
PHYLUM:	CHORDATA
CLASS:	MAMMALIA
ORDER:	CARNIVORA
FAMILY:	MUSTELIDAE
GENUS:	GULO
SPECIES:	G. GULO

MEPHITIDAE

Skunks

The Mephitidae family is made up of twelve species, including skunks and stink badgers. Members of this family are known for warding off predators using their highly developed anal scent glands.

ESTIMATED NUMBER OF MEPHITIDAE SPECIES 12

DID YOU KNOW? *Even though they have similar scent glands to the mustelids, skunks are closer related to raccoons.*

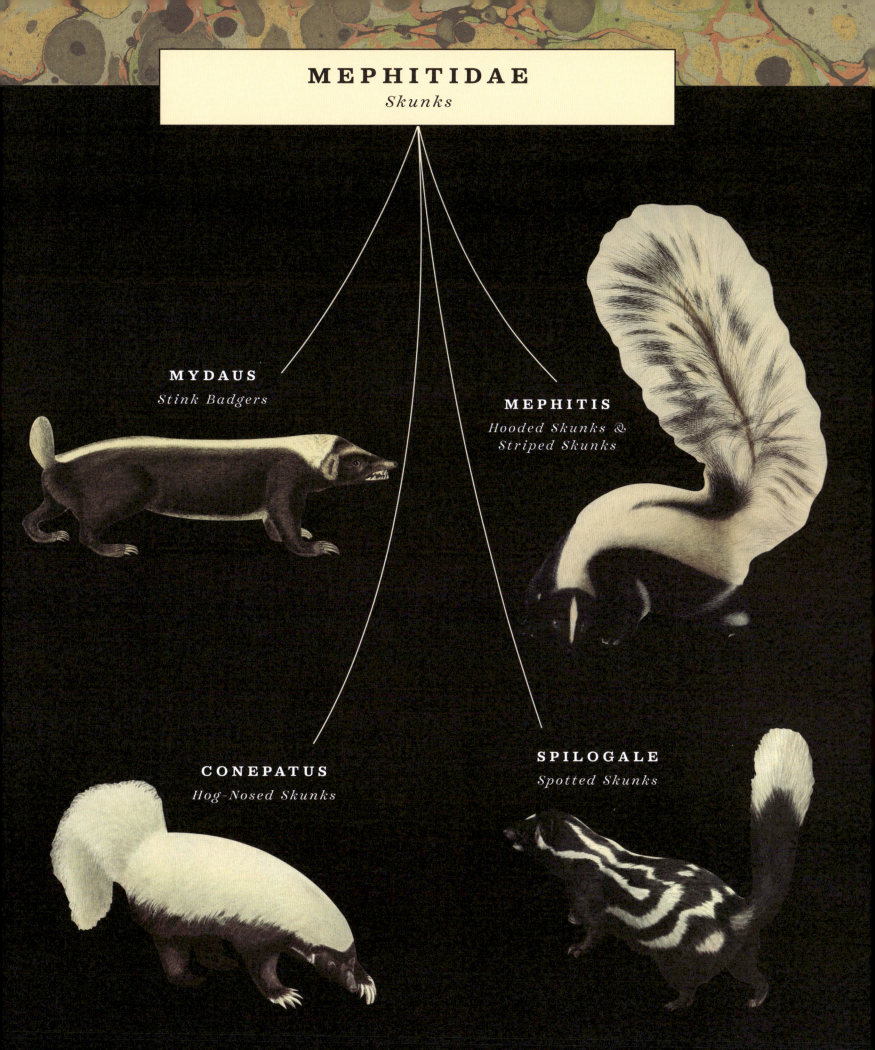

STRIPED SKUNK *Mephitis mephitis*

CONSERVATION STATUS: LEAST CONCERN

Striped skunks live throughout the United States, southern Canada, and northern Mexico. They are easily identifiable by their black coat with two white stripes along their back and tail, in addition to a small stripe on their forehead. Each stripe and color pattern is unique and varies by the individual. When striped skunks are upset or feel threatened, they stomp their feet, arch their back, and raise their tail. This acts as a warning before they spray a yellowish musk from two scent glands located at the base of their tail.

BY THE NUMBERS	
10 FEET	Reach of spray
1.5 MILES	Radius that spray can be smelled
0.5 MILES	Distance a striped skunk will travel from home

CLASSIFICATION	
KINGDOM:	ANIMALIA
PHYLUM:	CHORDATA
CLASS:	MAMMALIA
ORDER:	CARNIVORA
FAMILY:	MEPHITIDAE
GENUS:	MEPHITIS
SPECIES:	M. MEPHITIS

SMELLY CLIMBERS

Eastern spotted skunks are the only variety of skunk that has the ability to climb.

EASTERN SPOTTED SKUNK *Spilogale putorius*

CONSERVATION STATUS: VULNERABLE	BY THE NUMBERS		CLASSIFICATION
Eastern spotted skunks live in wooded areas, tall grass prairies, and rocky habitats. They seek shelter in burrows or dens that are abandoned by other animals or build their own. They rest most of the winter, but are not truly nocturnal animals, as they come out on mild-weathered days to eat. They are omnivores and eat a variety of plants and animals depending on the season. When eastern spotted skunks feel threatened, they will do a handstand and stomp their feet.	**10** YEARS	Lifespan	**KINGDOM:** ANIMALIA
	14–18 INCHES	Length	**PHYLUM:** CHORDATA
			CLASS: MAMMALIA
			ORDER: CARNIVORA
			FAMILY: MEPHITIDAE
	1.5 POUNDS	Weight	**GENUS:** SPILOGALE
			SPECIES: S. PUTORIUS

PROCYONIDAE

Raccoons and Other Procyonids

The Procyonidae family is made of fourteen species, all omnivores. Procyonids are known for being smart and having problem-solving abilities. Many also have ringed or banded tails with species-specific facial markings.

ESTIMATED NUMBER OF PROCYONIDAE SPECIES: 14

DID YOU KNOW? In German, the procyonids are considered bears. For instance the word for raccoon is Waschbär, which literally means "Wash Bear."

COMMON RACCOON *Procyon lotor*

CONSERVATION STATUS: LEAST CONCERN

Common raccoons are also known as northern racoons or Guadeloupe racoons. They are the largest member of the Procyonidae family and are most distinguishable for their black mask and long banded tail. They have long, slender front paws that are very dexterous, allowing them to climb, grab, hold, and pull things apart. Common raccoons are widely distributed, living in both forested and urban areas. They are typically nocturnal animals, foraging for food at night. Raccoons live in dens with other members of the same sex.

BY THE NUMBERS	
4–10	Rings per tail
180°	Rotation of hind feet
33%	Amount of diet that is plants

CLASSIFICATION
KINGDOM: ANIMALIA
PHYLUM: CHORDATA
CLASS: MAMMALIA
ORDER: CARNIVORA
FAMILY: PROCYONIDAE
GENUS: PROCYON
SPECIES: P. LOTOR

RING-TAILED RICOCHET

Ring-tailed cats are excellent climbers with great agility and can maneuver and ricochet along canyon walls. Ring-tailed cats use their long tail to balance on narrow branches and ledges. If they get in a tight spot, they can cartwheel backward to reverse direction.

RING-TAILED CAT *Bassariscus astutus*

CONSERVATION STATUS: LEAST CONCERN

Ring-tailed cats, also known simply as ringtails, are small members of the racoon family that resemble a fox or house cat. They most commonly live in hot, rocky terrain near water, such as in riparian canyons, caves, and even mine shafts.

BY THE NUMBERS	
10–12 INCHES	*Tail length*
180°	*Hindfoot ankle rotation*
14–16	*Number of black-and-white rings on tail*

CLASSIFICATION
KINGDOM: ANIMALIA
PHYLUM: CHORDATA
CLASS: MAMMALIA
ORDER: CARNIVORA
FAMILY: PROCYONIDAE
GENUS: BASSARISCUS
SPECIES: B. ASTUTUS

SOUTH AMERICAN COATI *Nasua nasua*

CONSERVATION STATUS: LEAST CONCERN

South American coatis live in tropical and subtropical regions of South America. Their coloring varies from gray to reddish to light or dark brown, and the rings on some individuals may be very faded. South American coatis are generally land animals, though they do spend a lot of time in the trees sleeping, mating, and giving birth. They can descend trees headfirst by reversing the joints in their ankle bone. They will typically only use this method if disturbed or escaping a predator, as they prefer to descend limb by limb.

BY THE NUMBERS	
6.61–13.22 POUNDS	*Weight*
3–7	*Cubs per litter*
7–8 YEARS	*Lifespan*

CLASSIFICATION

- **KINGDOM:** Animalia
- **PHYLUM:** Chordata
- **CLASS:** Mammalia
- **ORDER:** Carnivora
- **FAMILY:** Procyonidae
- **GENUS:** Nasua
- **SPECIES:** N. nasua

KINKAJOU *Potos flavus*

CONSERVATION STATUS: LEAST CONCERN

Kinkajous are a nocturnal species that live in tropical rainforests from southern Mexico to Brazil. They are nicknamed "honey bears" because they often raid beehives using their long, skinny tongue to gather honey. They are primarily classified as carnivores because they have canine teeth but generally have a frugivorous diet. They eat a variety of seasonal fruits, with figs being their favorite. Kinkajous have a prehensile tail with short hair, which acts similar to a fifth hand for balance and support in the tree canopy. They have flexible spines that allow them to curl up to sleep in palm trees or tree hollows during the day.

BY THE NUMBERS	
7:00 P.M.–12:00 A.M.	*Peak activity*
3–6 WEEKS OLD	*Tail becomes prehensile*
90%	*Percent of fruit in their diet*

CLASSIFICATION

KINGDOM: Animalia
PHYLUM: Chordata
CLASS: Mammalia
ORDER: Carnivora
FAMILY: Procyonidae
SUBFAMILY: Potosinae
GENUS: Potos
SPECIES: P. flavus

FELIDAE

Cats

The Felidae family is made up of thirty-six species, ranging in body size from small to large. Other common characteristics include facial whiskers, protractible claws, round heads with flat faces, tongues covered in papillae, and large eyes and ears. Members of this family may also be referred to as felids.

ESTIMATED NUMBER OF FELIDAE SPECIES | **36**

DID YOU KNOW? *All Felidae are carnivores and predators, preferring to stalk and ambush their prey.*

FELIDAE
Cats

PANTHERINAE

PANTHERA
Leopards, Lions, Jaguars & Tigers

NEOFELIS
Clouded Leopards

FELINAE

PARDOFELIS
Marbled Cats

CATOPUMA
Bay Cats & Asian Golden Cats

CARACAL
Caracals & African Golden Cats

LYNX
Lynxes & Bobcats

LEPTAILURUS
Servals

HERPAILURUS
Jaguarundis

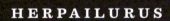

LEOPARDUS
Ocelots, Margays, Pamas Cats, Andean Mountain Cats, Kodkods, Oncillas & Geoffroy's Cats

PUMA
Cougars

PRIONAILURUS
Leopard Cats, Fishing Cats, Flat-Headed Cats & Rusty-Spotted Cats

ACINONYX
Cheetahs

FELIS
Jungle Cats, Black-Footed Cats, Sand Cats, Wildcats, Chinese Mountain Cats & Domestic Cats

OTOCOLOBUS
Pallas's Cats

AFRICAN LION *Panthera leo*
ASIATIC LION *Panthera leo ssp. persica*

CONSERVATION STATUS: VULNERABLE & ENDANGERED

Asiatic lions are a subspecies of African lions. Asiatic lions only live in Gir National Park in India. This subspecies is notable for being smaller in size, having a smaller, thinner mane, and living in smaller prides. African lions, however, live within a variety of habitats within sub-Saharan Africa, excluding the desert and rainforest. Although they are larger in size and weight than Asiatic lions, their substantial mane also gives them a very intimidating appearance to predators.

BY THE NUMBERS	
50 MILES PER HOUR	Top speed
36 FEET	Leaping distance
1,000 POUNDS	Largest sized animal a lion can kill

CLASSIFICATION

- KINGDOM: ANIMALIA
- PHYLUM: CHORDATA
- CLASS: MAMMALIA
- ORDER: CARNIVORA
- SUBORDER: FELIFORMIA
- FAMILY: FELIDAE
- SUBFAMILY: PANTHERINAE
- GENUS: PANTHERA
- SPECIES: P. LEO
- SUBSPECIES: P. L. LEO

LION LABOR

Generally, females do most of the hunting while the males protect the pride. This is standard for both African and Asiatic lions.

SNOW LEOPARD *Panthera uncia*

CONSERVATION STATUS: VULNERABLE

Snow leopards reside in the high mountains of Central and South Asia. They have particularly long tails that are used for balance on the steep, rocky terrain, as well as for extra warmth to wrap around themselves in the cold. They have large paws that are believed to be an adaptation for walking on snow. Snow leopards are solitary animals that live alone and don't socialize with others, except during mating season or with their mothers as cubs. They are most active at dawn and dusk each day, when they hunt their prey by stalking and ambushing from above off an elevated surface or ledge.

BY THE NUMBERS	
9,842– 14,763 FEET	Habitat elevation
2.3 MILLION SQUARE KILOMETERS	Geographic range
75– 90%	Percent of total body length that is the tail

CLASSIFICATION
KINGDOM: ANIMALIA
PHYLUM: CHORDATA
CLASS: MAMMALIA
ORDER: CARNIVORA
SUBORDER: FELIFORMIA
FAMILY: FELIDAE
SUBFAMILY: PANTHERINAE
GENUS: PANTHERA
SPECIES: P. UNCIA

MOUNTAIN MEALS

Snow leopards are carnivores that favor blue sheep, ibex, markhors, Himalayan tahr, wild goats, and wild boars.

AFRICAN LEOPARD *Panthera pardus pardus*

CONSERVATION STATUS: LEAST CONCERN

African leopards live in sub-Saharan Africa in a variety of habitats, including deserts, grasslands, and tropical forests. They spend a great deal of their time in the canopy of trees, where they avoid potential dangers from other predators. They are generally nocturnal, solitary animals that eat a variety of medium-sized mammals, but they will also eat reptiles, birds, and sometimes insects. When they get a large kill, they take the meat up a tree to protect it, using their specially attached shoulder blades to help lift. African leopards have a coat covered in rosettes that look similar to small roses. Unlike other felids, African leopards do not have any spots inside the rosettes.

BY THE NUMBERS	
58 MILES PER HOUR	Top speed
19.7 FEET	Leaping distance
10–12 YEARS	Lifespan

CLASSIFICATION

- **KINGDOM:** Animalia
- **PHYLUM:** Chordatav
- **CLASS:** Mammalia
- **ORDER:** Carnivora
- **SUBORDER:** Feliformia
- **FAMILY:** Felidae
- **SUBFAMILY:** Pantherinae
- **GENUS:** Panthera
- **SPECIES:** P. pardus
- **SUBSPECIES:** P. p. pardus

BENGAL TIGER *Panthera tigris tigris*

CONSERVATION STATUS: ENDANGERED

Bengal tigers are one of six remaining subspecies of Panthera tigris. They are located in parts of India, Bangladesh, Bhutan, Nepal, and China. They adapt well to both hot and cold habitats and live in mangroves, forests, and wetlands. A tiger's stripes are unique to the individual. Some may possess a recessive, mutant genetic condition that creates a white coat with stripes.

BY THE NUMBERS	
88 POUNDS	*Maximum amount of meat eaten in one meal*
4 INCHES	*Length of teeth*
2,000	*Estimated Bengal tigers remaining*

CLASSIFICATION	
KINGDOM:	Animalia
PHYLUM:	Chordata
CLASS:	Mammalia
ORDER:	Carnivora
SUBORDER:	Feliformia
FAMILY:	Felidae
SUBFAMILY:	Pantherinae
GENUS:	Panthera
SPECIES:	P. tigris
SUBSPECIES:	P. t. tigris

TIGER TRAPS

Bengal tigers are solitary animals, spending most of their days resting in the shade, conserving energy until it is time to hunt. They are carnivores and prey on animals such as water buffalo, deer, gaur, and boar. They stalk their prey from behind and quietly ambush them.

NORTH AMERICAN COUGAR *Puma concolor couguar*

CONSERVATION STATUS: LEAST CONCERN

North American cougars live in habitats with rocky mountains and forests. They find shelter in caves, rock or fallen tree crevices, and even large bushes. North American cougars typically hunt only twice a week and usually do so at nighttime. They are carnivores who eat mostly deer, coyotes, beavers, porcupines, and other animals. They will stalk their prey and ambush from behind while biting their neck, causing suffocation.

BY THE NUMBERS	
18 FEET	*Jumping distance straight into the air*
30–40 FEET	*Jumping distance horizontally into the air*
33.5 MILES PER HOUR	*Top speed*

CLASSIFICATION

- KINGDOM: ANIMALIA
- PHYLUM: CHORDATA
- CLASS: MAMMALIA
- ORDER: CARNIVORA
- SUBORDER: FELIFORMIA
- FAMILY: FELIDAE
- SUBFAMILY: FELINAE
- GENUS: PUMA
- SPECIES: P. CONCOLOR
- SUBSPECIES: P. C. COUGUAR

JAGUAR *Panthera onca*

CONSERVATION STATUS: NEAR THREATENED

Jaguars are the largest felid in the Americas and Western Hemisphere. They live in New Mexico and Arizona and on south to Argentina in a variety of habitats, including deserts, grasslands, and tropical forests. They prefer to live near a water source, such as a river, lake, or stream, as they are excellent swimmers. Jaguars can be misidentified as leopards; however, a jaguar's fur has a spot in the center of each rosette. They are also, overall, stockier with more muscle compared to leopards. Black jaguars, sometimes referred to as black panthers, get their black coloring, called melanism, from a single dominant allele in their gene pool. Jaguars kill their prey by stalking and ambushing, with a fatal bite to the skull.

BY THE NUMBERS	
6%	Percentage of jaguars that are melanistic (black)
85 SPECIES	Jaguar's prey
50–60%	Percentage of each day a jaguar is active

CLASSIFICATION

KINGDOM: ANIMALIA
PHYLUM: CHORDATA
CLASS: MAMMALIA
ORDER: CARNIVORA
SUBORDER: FELIFORMIA
FAMILY: FELIDAE
SUBFAMILY: PANTHERINAE
GENUS: PANTHERA
SPECIES: P. ONCAE

BOBCAT *Lynx rufus*

CONSERVATION STATUS: VULNERABLE

Bobcats live in southern Canada, the United States, and Mexico. Sometimes they can be confused with other lynx species, but bobcats live in warmer habitats, are smaller, and usually have tan or brown fur with dark stripes and spots. Their darker coat helps camouflage them among rocks and vegetation. This is helpful while hunting for prey, which they stalk and then pounce on and bite the vertebrae on the neck, killing the animal (usually a rabbit or hare). Bobcats have two white spots on the back of each ear, which kittens use to follow their mother in low lighting. They also have white on the underside of their tail and, similarly, if the kittens fall behind, the mother will raise her tail while calling for them so they can spot and follow her.

BY THE NUMBERS	
30 MILES PER HOUR	*Top speed*
2–7 MILES	*Distance traveled while stalking prey*
3	*Kittens per litter*

CLASSIFICATION	
KINGDOM:	Animalia
PHYLUM:	Chordata
CLASS:	Mammalia
ORDER:	Carnivora
SUBORDER:	Feliformia
FAMILY:	Felidae
SUBFAMILY:	Felinae
GENUS:	Lynx
SPECIES:	L. rufus

CARACAL *Caracal caracal*

CONSERVATION STATUS: LEAST CONCERN	BY THE NUMBERS		CLASSIFICATION
Caracals are sometimes referred to as desert lynxes because of their ear tufts; however, they are not a lynx species at all. Caracals live in Africa, Central Asia, and southwestern Asia. They are known for their jumping abilities to catch birds midair as well as for their beautiful, sleek appearance with a reddish-brown coat. Caracals use their fur coats as a main defense mechanism against predators. If they feel threatened, they will lay down flat and camouflage among the dirt and rocks to avoid detection.	**10** FEET	*Leaping distance*	KINGDOM: ANIMALIA
			PHYLUM: CHORDATA
			CLASS: MAMMALIA
	32–55 INCHES	*Average body and tail length*	ORDER: CARNIVORA
			SUBORDER: FELIFORMIA
			FAMILY: FELIDAE
	90%	*Percent of fruit in their diet*	SUBFAMILY: FELINAE
			GENUS: CARACAL
			SPECIES: C. CARACAL

CANIDAE

Wolves, Dogs, and Foxes

The Canidae family is made up of thirty-four species, including coyotes, dogs, foxes, jackals, and wolves. Members of this family are called canids.

ESTIMATED NUMBER OF CANIDAE SPECIES 34

DID YOU KNOW? *Canidae are found on all continents but Antarctica. They arrived independently or accompanied by humans.*

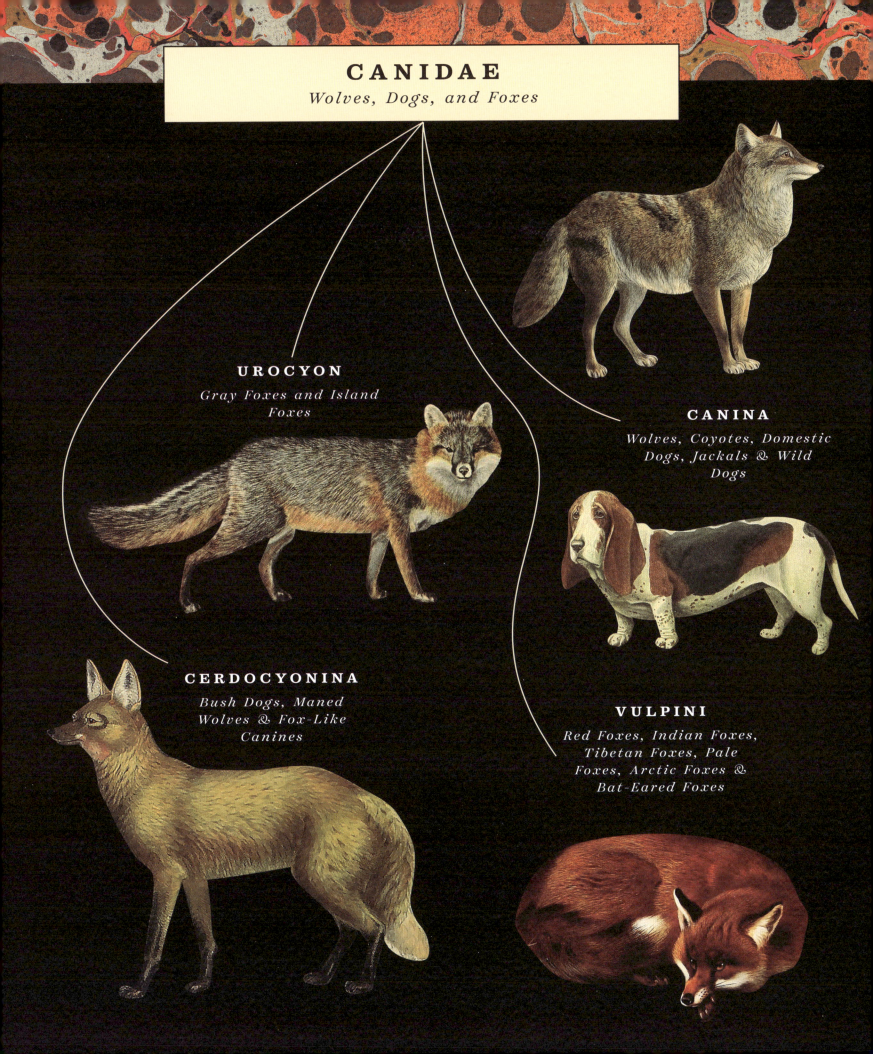

ETHIOPIAN WOLF *Canis simensis*

CONSERVATION STATUS: ENDANGERED

Ethiopian wolves are found in only a few select mountain ranges in Ethiopia. They live in packs, where they socialize and protect the border of their territory. Each pack has a hierarchy for both males and females, and both dominant or submissive behavior is displayed within the pack.

BY THE NUMBERS	
9,842–14,435 FEET	Habitat elevation
3–13	Pack size
2.3 SQUARE MILES	Pack territory size

CLASSIFICATION
KINGDOM: ANIMALIA
PHYLUM: CHORDATA
CLASS: MAMMALIA
ORDER: CARNIVORA
FAMILY: CANIDAE
GENUS: CANIS
SPECIES: C. SIMENSIS

LONE WOLVES

Interestingly, Ethiopian wolves typically do not hunt in packs, but instead hunt and eat individually. Their diet consists of a variety of rodents and they will dig them out of their burrows to eat.

PLAINS COYOTE *Canis latrans latrans*

CONSERVATION STATUS: LEAST CONCERN

Plains coyotes are also sometimes known as prairie wolves or brush wolves. They are the largest coyote subspecies, known for their downward pointing tail. Plains coyotes are mostly nocturnal, coming out in the dark to forage. Their diet primarily consists of hares and deer. Plains coyotes mate between January and March and give birth to a litter of pups inside a burrow. The pups will be cared for by both parents until they are independent, around six to nine months old.

BY THE NUMBERS	
40 MILES PER HOUR	Top speed
4–7	Pups per litter
5–7 WEEKS	Age of weaning

CLASSIFICATION

KINGDOM: ANIMALIA
PHYLUM: CHORDATA
CLASS: MAMMALIA
ORDER: CARNIVORA
FAMILY: CANIDAE
GENUS: CANIS
SPECIES: C. LATRANS

DINGO *Canis lupus dingo*

CONSERVATION STATUS: NOT EVALUATED

Dingoes live in Australia and parts of Southeast Asia. They look similar to domestic dogs but differ in their lean body, bushy tail, longer canine teeth, and longer, tapered muzzle. Generally, dingoes live in packs that they stay in from birth. Dingoes are known for pairing off and mating for life. Within the pack, there is a dominant couple that has authority over the remainder of the pack; however, the dominant male also has power over the dominant female. Breeding is very limited within each pack, and if another female in the pack becomes pregnant, the dominant female will kill her cubs.

BY THE NUMBERS	
3–12	Pack size
5–6	Pups per litter
1	Litter per pack, per year

CLASSIFICATION

- **KINGDOM:** Animalia
- **PHYLUM:** Chordata
- **CLASS:** Mammalia
- **ORDER:** Carnivora
- **FAMILY:** Canidae
- **GENUS:** Canis
- **SPECIES:** C. lupus
- **SUBSPECIES:** C. l. dingo

FOX TALK

Red foxes use a variety of tools to communicate with each other, including vocalizations, facial expressions, and scent markings through urine, feces, and other secretions.

RED FOX *Vulpes vulpes*

CONSERVATION STATUS: LEAST CONCERN

Red foxes are the largest of the fox species, with males being slightly larger than females. They are widely distributed, living in a variety of habitats throughout North America, Europe, Asia, and parts of North Africa. They are solitary animals that do not form packs; however, they do at times live in family groups consisting of a male, one or two females, and their offspring. These family groups live in dens or burrows, where they protect and rear their offspring. Red foxes have an excellent sense of hearing, smell, touch, and sight that they use while hunting for mice and other prey.

BY THE NUMBERS	
6.61–30.84 POUNDS	Weight
100 FEET	Distance they can hear a mouse squeak
8	Vocalizations for communication

CLASSIFICATION	
KINGDOM:	ANIMALIA
PHYLUM:	CHORDATA
CLASS:	MAMMALIA
ORDER:	CARNIVORA
FAMILY:	CANIDAE
GENUS:	VULPES
SPECIES:	V. VULPES

ARCTIC FOX *Vulpes lagopus*

CONSERVATION STATUS: LEAST CONCERN

Arctic foxes live in the coastal regions of the Arctic tundra, anywhere north of the Arctic circle. This includes countries such as Canada, Russia, Europe, Greenland, and Iceland. Arctic foxes are opportunistic animals that eat a variety of small mammals, insects, berries, or carrion (decaying flesh of dead animals). They will hide food in their dens during summer to save for the harsh winter months.

BY THE NUMBERS	
5–8	Kits (babies) per litter
2	Litters per year
7–10 YEARS	Lifespan

CLASSIFICATION

- **KINGDOM:** ANIMALIA
- **PHYLUM:** CHORDATA
- **CLASS:** MAMMALIA
- **ORDER:** CARNIVORA
- **FAMILY:** CANIDAE
- **GENUS:** VULPES
- **SPECIES:** V. LAGOPUS

FASHIONABLE FOXES

Arctic foxes have unique fur that is white in the winter and blends in with the snow. Leading up to summer, they shed their fluffy coats for a thinner, brownish-gray coat that helps them camouflage among the rocky terrain after snowmelt.

AFRICAN WILD DOG *Lycaon pictus*

CONSERVATION STATUS: ENDANGERED

African wild dogs, also known as African painted dogs, are native to sub-Saharan Africa and live in grassland, savanna, and open woodland habitats. They have a bristle-like coat that thins with age, sometimes becoming so sparse they are nearly naked. Their spotted pattern is unique to each individual and acts as an identifying trait. African wild dogs live in packs with a dominant male and female couple. They work together to hunt, following the alpha male's lead, and track their prey until it gets tired, then attack and kill it. They prey on animals such as the kudu, gazelle, impala, bushbuck, and wildebeest.

BY THE NUMBERS

7–15	Average pack size
2–5 MINUTES	Time it takes to kill medium size prey
60–90%	Percentage of chases that end in a kill

CLASSIFICATION

KINGDOM: ANIMALIA
PHYLUM: CHORDATA
CLASS: MAMMALIA
ORDER: CARNIVORA
FAMILY: CANIDAE
SUBFAMILY: CANINAE
TRIBE: CANINI
GENUS: LYCAON
SPECIES: L. PICTUS

PINNIPEDIA

Seals

The Pinnipedia clade consists of three families and thirty-three species. All members of the Pinnipedia clade have four webbed flippers, eyesight and hearing developed for use in both air and water, a layer of blubber (fat) under their skin for warmth, and whiskers that are used as tactile sensors.

ESTIMATED NUMBER OF PINNIPEDIA SPECIES

33

DID YOU KNOW?

Pinnipeds have so much blubber that they can only tolerate cold water. As a result, they are absent from the warm Indian Ocean.

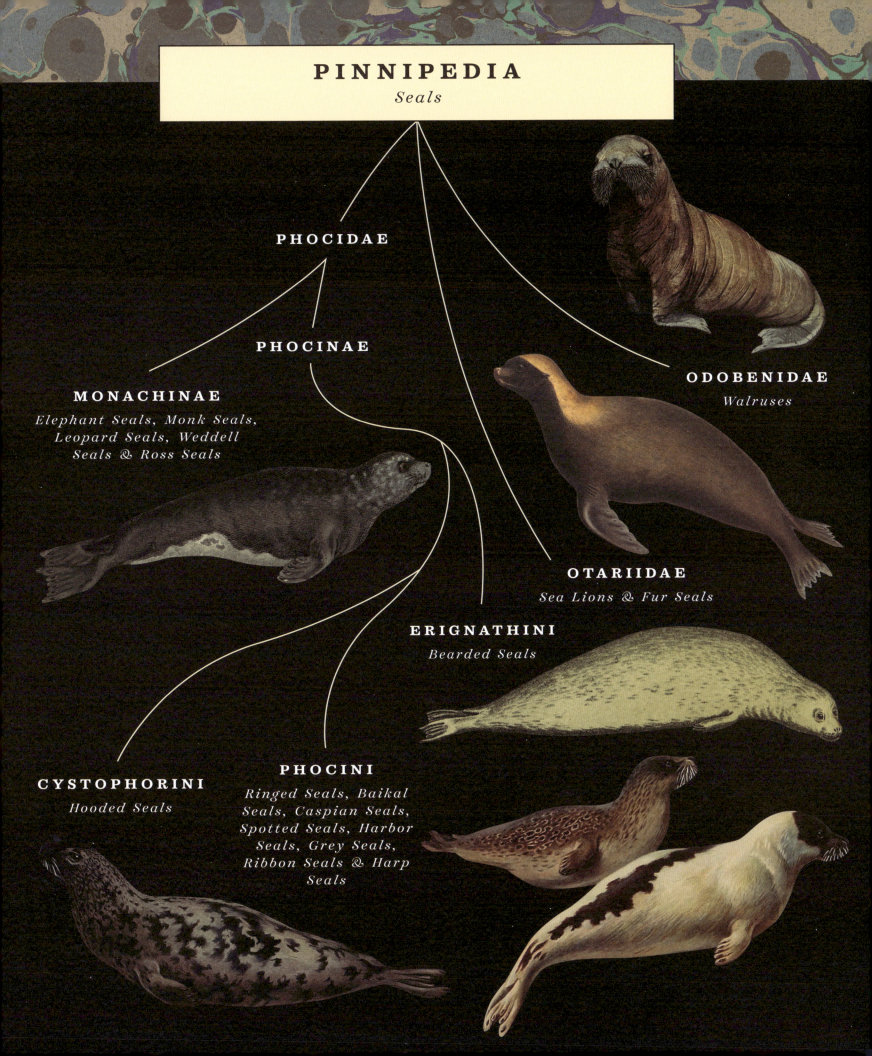

BEARDED SEAL *Erignathus barbatus*

CONSERVATION STATUS: LEAST CONCERN

Bearded seals live in the Arctic Ocean in shallow waters with pack ice. They get their name from their long whiskers that resemble a beard. These whiskers are sensitive and used to locate food by feeling for it. Bearded seals primarily eat mollusks, crustaceans, and arctic cod. They spend a great deal of their time floating on ice floes.

BY THE NUMBERS	
575–800 POUNDS	*Weight*
7–8 FEET	*Length*
325 FEET	*Diving depth for foraging*

CLASSIFICATION

- KINGDOM: Animalia
- PHYLUM: Chordata
- CLASS: Mammalia
- ORDER: Carnivora
- CLADE: Pinnipedia
- FAMILY: Phocidae
- GENUS: Erignathus
- SPECIES: E. barbatus

SOLO SEALS

Bearded seals are solitary animals that live alone, except during mating season.

RINGED SEAL *Pusa hispida*

CONSERVATION STATUS: LEAST CONCERN

Ringed seals get their name from the dark spots surrounded by gray rings on their backs. They are the smallest and most common Arctic seal. They do not have ears, and they have very strong claws used for cutting thick ice for breathing holes. They eat a very wide variety of fish and invertebrates, mostly mysids, shrimp, arctic cod, and herring.

BY THE NUMBERS	
6 FEET	*Ice thickness they can cut with their claws*
150 FEET	*Diving depth*
25–30 YEARS	*Lifespan*

CLASSIFICATION	
KINGDOM:	ANIMALIA
PHYLUM:	CHORDATA
CLASS:	MAMMALIA
ORDER:	CARNIVORA
CLADE:	PINNIPEDIA
FAMILY:	PHOCIDAE
GENUS:	PUSA
SPECIES:	P. HISPIDA

SEAL HUNTERS

Ringed seals face two main predators: polar bears and killer whales.

HARBOR SEAL *Phoca vitulina*

CONSERVATION STATUS: LEAST CONCERN

Harbor seals have a large geographical range and are one of the most common marine animals along US coasts. They have a variety of fur colors, including dark brown, tan, or gray—each with a lighter underside. Harbor seals are mostly solitary animals, but they haul out (rest) together on land when they are not foraging or traveling to regulate their body temperature, molt, give birth, or nurse their pups (babies). Hauling out together provides greater protection to the group from predators.

BY THE NUMBERS	
24 POUNDS	*Birth weight*
298 FEET	*Diving depth*
40 YEARS	*Lifespan*

CLASSIFICATION

- KINGDOM: ANIMALIA
- PHYLUM: CHORDATA
- CLASS: MAMMALIA
- ORDER: CARNIVORA
- CLADE: PINNIPEDIA
- FAMILY: PHOCIDAE
- GENUS: PHOCA
- SPECIES: P. VITULINA

FISH FOOD

Harbor Seals eat herring, anchovies, mackerel, cod, flatfish, and menhaden and will travel over 30 miles to find food.

HARP SEAL *Pagophilus groenlandicus*

CONSERVATION STATUS: LEAST CONCERN

Harp seals are found in the Arctic and northern Atlantic Oceans. Harp seal pups (babies) have lanugo, a long white fur that traps heat from the sun. This is important as the pups are born without any blubber (fat). They put on blubber from their mother's milk while nursing. Harp seals gather in large groups to rest on ice packs during molting and breeding season. They also travel long distances with these groups during migration.

BY THE NUMBERS

3–4 WEEKS	*Duration pups have lanugo*
5 POUNDS	*Weight gained per day nursing for first 12 days of life*
3,100 MILES	*Annual migration (roundtrip)*

CLASSIFICATION

- **KINGDOM:** Animalia
- **PHYLUM:** Chordata
- **CLASS:** Mammalia
- **ORDER:** Carnivora
- **CLADE:** Pinnipedia
- **FAMILY:** Phocidae
- **GENUS:** Pagophilus
- **SPECIES:** P. groenlandicus

COLD DRINKS

Harp seals eat ice and snow to stay hydrated. Their scientific name literally means "ice lover from Greenland."

AUSTRALIAN SEA LION *Neophoca cinerea*

CONSERVATION STATUS: ENDANGERED

Australian sea lions are only found on the water off Australia's coastlines. Males are very territorial and protect the borders of their territory from other males entering. Males show hostility through posture and aggressive behavior. A male keeps several females within his territory, and if a female strays, he will quickly herd her back. This leads to fights between males, as the female may move from one territory into another. Female Australian sea lions are known for their "fostering-like" behavior, when they protect and care for the offspring of another female while she is away, even adopting them as her own in severe cases where the mother is killed.

BY THE NUMBERS	
600 FEET	*Diving depth*
40 MINUTES	*Diving duration*
12 YEARS	*Lifespan*

CLASSIFICATION	
KINGDOM:	ANIMALIA
PHYLUM:	CHORDATA
CLASS:	MAMMALIA
ORDER:	CARNIVORA
CLADE:	PINNIPEDIA
FAMILY:	OTARIIDAE
GENUS:	NEOPHOCA
SPECIES:	N. CINEREA

WALRUS *Odobenus rosmarus*

CONSERVATION STATUS: VULNERABLE

The Latin name for walrus translates to "tooth-walking sea horse." It is a fitting name because both male and female walruses are known for their large tusks. These tusks are extended canine teeth and are used for breaking ice, pulling their large body out of the water onto the ice, as a defense mechanism, and as a way to establish dominance over other walruses. Typically, the older and larger the walrus is, the higher up it will be in the hierarchy; however, it must also be able to win in battle with its tusks to ensure that position. Tusk fights also occur between males as they fight over mating rights for females, and these fights can be deadly.

BY THE NUMBERS	
7.87 INCHES	*Thickness of ice that tusks can break through*
19.5 INCHES	*Average tusk length*
2,203 POUNDS	*Average weight*

CLASSIFICATION

KINGDOM: ANIMALIA
PHYLUM: CHORDATA
CLASS: MAMMALIA
ORDER: CARNIVORA
CLADE: PINNIPEDIA
FAMILY: ODOBENIDAE
GENUS: ODOBENUS
BRISSON, 1762
SPECIES: O. ROSMARUS

SIRENIA

Sea Cows

The Sirenia order is made of two families and four species. Members of the Sirenia family are almost completely hairless, have paddle-like front flippers and no external portion of their ears, and lack hind limbs.

ESTIMATED NUMBER OF SIRENIA SPECIES	4
DID YOU KNOW?	Sirenia comes from the word "sirens," the bewitching mermaids of Greek myth. Apparently sailors mistook dugongs for mermaids.

WEST INDIAN MANATEE
Trichechus manatus

CONSERVATION STATUS: VULNERABLE

West Indian manatees are also known as North American manatees or sea cows. They are most commonly found in shallow coastal areas near Florida and travel from Virginia to Texas in summer. They also can be found around the Caribbean, between Mexico and Brazil. They live in rivers, estuaries, and canals, as their bodies can adapt to large changes in salinity between freshwater and marine habitats. Because they have very little blubber, they stay in warmer tropical and subtropical waters.

BY THE NUMBERS		CLASSIFICATION	
6–8 HOURS	Time spent grazing for sea grasses	KINGDOM:	ANIMALIA
		PHYLUM:	CHORDATA
5–10% OF BODY WEIGHT	Daily food consumption	CLASS:	MAMMALIA
		ORDER:	SIRENIA
		FAMILY:	TRICHECHIDAE
440–1,320 POUNDS	Body weight range	GENUS:	TRICHECHUS
		SPECIES:	T. MANATUS

SEA GRASS FED

West Indian manatees are herbivores and graze on large quantities of sea grasses that grow on the ocean floor. The turn of their mouth helps aid them in grasping plants, but they will also use their flippers to dig up entire roots of plants.

SIRENIA
Sea Cows

TRICHECHIDAE
Amazonian Manatees, West Indian Manatees & African Manatees

DUGONGIDAE
Dugongs

DUGONG *Dugong dugon*

CONSERVATION STATUS: VULNERABLE

Dugongs live in shallow waters of the Pacific and Indian Oceans, from east Africa to the Red Sea and Australia. Unlike manatees, dugongs do not have the ability to live in freshwater. They are herbivores that graze on sea grasses. They are quite social and live in groups that range in size. These groups are sometimes nomadic, meaning they wander to find beds of sea grasses large enough to sustain their group and, when depleted, they travel to find a new one.

SIREN SONGS

Dugongs have excellent hearing and communicate with each other underwater using different sounds.

BY THE NUMBERS		CLASSIFICATION
18 MONTHS	Duration calves will nurse	**KINGDOM:** Animalia **PHYLUM:** Chordata **CLASS:** Mammalia **ORDER:** Sirenia **FAMILY:** Dugongidae **SUBFAMILY:** Dugonginae **GENUS:** Dugong **SPECIES:** D. dugon
32.81 FEET	Diving depth	
70 YEARS	Lifespan	

ELEPHANTIDAE

Elephants

The Elephantidae family is made up of three species. Members of this family have long trunks, big heads, cylinder-shaped legs, and flat ears.

ESTIMATED NUMBER OF ELEPHANTIDAE SPECIES 3

DID YOU KNOW? *Elephants are among the smartest of animals. They can recognize themselves in a mirror and use tools like flyswatters.*

ELEPHANTIDAE
Elephants

ELEPHAS
Sri Lankan Elephants, Indian Elephants, Sumatran Elephants & Borneo Elephants

LOXODONTA
African Bush Elephants & African Forest Elephants

AFRICAN ELEPHANT *Loxodonta*

CONSERVATION STATUS:
ENDANGERED (AFRICAN SAVANNA ELEPHANT) & CRITICALLY ENDANGERED (AFRICAN FOREST ELEPHANT)

African elephants are the largest living land mammal. They live in sub-Saharan Africa in deserts, forests, grasslands, and woodland habitats. African elephants, like all other types of elephants, live in matriarchal (female-led) groups. These groups communicate with each other through long distances by stomping their feet on the ground and feeling the vibrations, which can warn others of potential danger. African elephants will use their large ears to help hear distant sounds, as well as to cool down their body as each ear contains many blood vessels.

BY THE NUMBERS	
20 MILES	*Distance vibrations can be felt from stomping by other herds*
1.5 GALLONS	*Trunk suction capacity*
4,762–13,334 POUNDS	*Body weight range*

CLASSIFICATION
KINGDOM: Animalia
PHYLUM: Chordata
CLASS: Mammalia
ORDER: Proboscidea
FAMILY: Elephantidae
SUBFAMILY: Elephantinae
GENUS: Loxodonta

TOUGH TRUNKS

The trunk of African elephants has thousands of muscles that allow the animal to move it in all directions. African elephants do not drink through their trunk, but instead use it to suck up water and then squirt it into their mouth.

INDIAN ELEPHANT *Elephas maximus indicus*

CONSERVATION STATUS: ENDANGERED

Indian elephants are a subspecies of Asian elephants and found on mainland Asia. Their habitat includes grasslands and a variety of forests. Females are identifiable by their smaller size and have shorter or no tusks at all. Indian elephants are herbivores and consume very large quantities of grasses, legumes, palms, sedges, and other cultivated crops each day.

BY THE NUMBERS	
330 POUNDS	*Plant matter consumed daily*
19	*Hours of feeding each day*
4,400– 11,000 POUNDS	*Body weight range*

CLASSIFICATION

- KINGDOM: ANIMALIA
- PHYLUM: CHORDATA
- CLASS: MAMMALIA
- ORDER: PROBOSCIDEA
- FAMILY: ELEPHANTIDAE
- GENUS: ELEPHAS
- SPECIES: E. MAXIMUS
- SUBSPECIES: E. M. INDICUS

ELEPHANT GOVERNMENT

Indian elephants are social animals and live in groups of related females, with the oldest female being the leader. The leader guides her group to areas where there is adequate food and water.

ASIAN ELEPHANT *Elephas maximus*

CONSERVATION STATUS: ENDANGERED

Asian elephants live in small areas of India and southeast Asia in scrub forests and rainforests. Asian elephants have four hooves on their hind feet and the highest part of their body is their head. They spend a great deal of time foraging for food and try to regulate their body temperature by avoiding too much sunlight. They are often found in the shade, submerged in water, rolling in a mud bath, or spraying themselves with water to cool down.

BY THE NUMBERS	
2 HOURS	Amount of sleep per day
40–50 GALLONS	Daily water intake
4,405–13,216 POUNDS	Body weight range

CLASSIFICATION	
KINGDOM:	Animalia
PHYLUM:	Chordata
CLASS:	Mammalia
ORDER:	Proboscidea
FAMILY:	Elephantidae
GENUS:	Elephas
SPECIES:	E. maximus

SMALL GIANTS

Asian elephants are smaller in size than African elephants and have smaller ears. Additionally, they have only one prehensile "finger" at the tip of their trunk, which is used to grasp and lift objects. African elephants have two.

HYAENIDAE

Hyenas

The Hyaenidae family consists of four species. Members of this family have very large jaws with big molars and premolars that are used to crush the bones of their prey.

ESTIMATED NUMBER OF HYAENIDAE SPECIES	4
DID YOU KNOW?	Not all hyenas are scavengers. Spotted hyenas are hunters, and aardwolfs are insectivores.

STRIPED HYENA

Hyaena hyaena

CONSERVATION STATUS: NEAR THREATENED

Striped hyenas live in Northern and Eastern Africa, the Middle East, and India in semi-deserts, rocky scrublands, and savanna habitats. They are identifiable by their black stripes as well as a mane that extends down their back. This mane can be raised to make them appear bigger in efforts to scare off predators. Striped hyenas have taller front legs than back legs, which give the appearance that they are limping uphill when they walk.

BY THE NUMBERS		CLASSIFICATION	
38%	Size increase with raised mane	KINGDOM:	ANIMALIA
		PHYLUM:	CHORDATA
		CLASS:	MAMMALIA
1–6	Cubs per litter	ORDER:	CARNIVORA
		SUBORDER:	FELIFORMIA
2X	Heart size compared to similar sized mammals	FAMILY:	HYAENIDAE
		SUBFAMILY:	HYAENINAE
		GENUS:	HYAENA
		SPECIES:	H. HYAENA

SINGLE LADIES

Striped hyenas are rather quiet and do not make the laughing or cackling sound that other hyena species are known for. They are mostly solitary animals, but occasionally live in small groups of one female and several males, as females have dominance over males.

HYAENIDAE
Hyenas & Aardwolves

HYAENINAE
Striped, Spotted, & Cave Hyenas

PROTELINAE
Aardwolves

BROWN HYENA
Parahyaena brunnea

CONSERVATION STATUS: NEAR THREATENED

The brown hyena lives in the southern regions of Africa in desert, semi-desert, open woodland savanna, and grassland habitats. They are easily identifiable from other hyena species because of their long, shaggy hair and pointed ears. Generally, brown hyenas are opportunistic feeders that hunt alone, foraging for carrion (decaying flesh of dead animals) or the carcass remains other large carnivores leave from their kills. They also bury leftover food under shrubs to eat the following day.

BY THE NUMBERS		CLASSIFICATION
21.7 MILES	Nightly distance traveled while foraging	**KINGDOM:** Animalia **PHYLUM:** Chordata **CLASS:** Mammalia **ORDER:** Carnivora **SUBORDER:** Feliformia **FAMILY:** Hyaenidae **GENUS:** Parahyaena **SPECIES:** P. brunnea
31 MILES PER HOUR	Top speed	
12–13 YEARS	Life expectancy	

FRUIT FOOD

Hyenas are nocturnal and sleep in dens under the cover of bushes, trees, or rocks to avoid becoming overheated. Brown hyenas also eat fruit with high water content to be able to survive hot, dry conditions.

PRIMATES

Monkeys and Apes

The Primate order is made of roughly 521 species. Members of the Primate order have prehensile five-digit hands, feet with flat nails, eyes that face forward, vision that is more important than smell, and collarbones.

ESTIMATED NUMBER OF PRIMATES SPECIES	**521**
DID YOU KNOW?	*Primates have larger brains than most animals, and many primates make frequent use of tools.*

PRIMATES
Monkeys and Apes

STREPSIRRHINI **HAPLORHINI**

LORISOIDEA
Lorisids & Galagos

LEMUROIDEA
Lemurs

ATELIDAE
Howler Monkeys, Spider Monkeys & Woolly Monkeys

TARSIIDAE
Tarsiers

CALLITRICHIDAE
Marmosets & Tamarins

HOMINIDAE
Great Apes

PITHECIIDAE
Titis, Sakis & Uakaris

CEBIDAE
Capuchins & Squirrel Monkeys

HYLOBATIDAE
Gibbons

AOTIDAE
Owl Monkeys

CERCOPITHECIDAE
Old World Monkeys

EASTERN GORILLA *Gorilla beringei*

CONSERVATION STATUS: CRITICALLY ENDANGERED

Eastern gorillas live in regions of the Virunga volcanoes between the Democratic Republic of Congo, Rwanda, and Uganda, as well as in the Bwindi Impenetrable National Park in Uganda. Eastern gorillas are the largest primates in the world, with males being larger than females. They are identifiable from other gorilla species by their longer hair, shorter arms, bigger jaws and teeth, and smaller nose. The males are sometimes referred to as silverbacks because of an area of hair on their back that is silver-gray in color.

BY THE NUMBERS	
30%	Daily time spent feeding
30%	Daily time spent traveling
40%	Daily time spent resting

CLASSIFICATION

- KINGDOM: ANIMALIA
- PHYLUM: CHORDATA
- CLASS: MAMMALIA
- ORDER: PRIMATES
- SUBORDER: HAPLORHINI
- INFRAORDER: SIMIIFORMES
- FAMILY: HOMINIDAE
- SUBFAMILY: HOMININAE
- GENUS: GORILLA
- SPECIES: G. BERINGEI

GORILLA FAMILIES

Eastern gorillas live in social groups with one male, multiple females, and their offspring. They are classified as semi-terrestrial because they live, sleep, and play on both land and in the treetops.

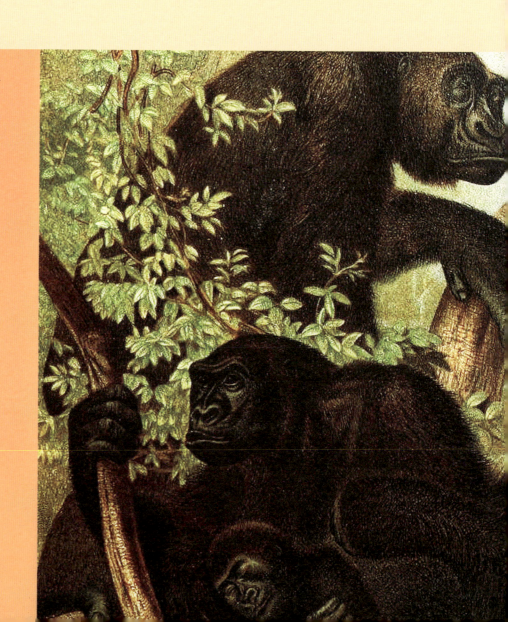

CHIMPANZEE *Pan troglodytes*

CONSERVATION STATUS: ENDANGERED

Chimpanzees, called chimps for short, live in western and central Africa in savannas and tropical rainforests. Baby chimpanzees (infants) form tight bonds with their mothers. As infants, they can be found hanging from their mother's underside, and later on their mother's back as they learn to walk. Chimpanzees are very social and live in community groups but sometimes travel in sub-groups or alone.

BY THE NUMBERS	
12–15 YEARS OLD	*First time a female gives birth*
4 YEARS OLD	*Infants learn to walk*
6–10	*Community group size*

CLASSIFICATION	
KINGDOM:	Animalia
PHYLUM:	Chordata
CLASS:	Mammalia
ORDER:	Primates
SUBORDER:	Haplorhini
INFRAORDER:	Simiiformes
FAMILY:	Hominidae
SUBFAMILY:	Homininae
TRIBE:	Hominini
GENUS:	Pan
SPECIES:	P. troglodytes

TERMITE TOOLS

Chimpanzees are known for their high intelligence, memory and communication skills, and ability to make and use tools from a young age, which aid in acquiring food. For example, chimpanzees will put a stick into an ant or termite hill to collect the insects to eat.

BORNEAN ORANGUTAN *Pongo pygmaeus*

CONSERVATION STATUS: CRITICALLY ENDANGERED

Bornean orangutans get their name from the island of Borneo, where they live in Southeast Asia. Bornean orangutans mostly live alone, with the exception of mothers and their offspring, as they are not social animals. They spend most of their time in the trees, where they build a new nest to sleep each night.

BY THE NUMBERS	
7 FEET	*Adult male arm span*
15–20 YEARS OLD	*Male becomes flanged*
50 YEARS	*Lifespan*

CLASSIFICATION
KINGDOM: ANIMALIA
PHYLUM: CHORDATA
CLASS: MAMMALIA
ORDER: PRIMATES
SUBORDER: HAPLORHINI
INFRAORDER: SIMIIFORMES
FAMILY: HOMINIDAE
GENUS: PONGO
SPECIES: P. PYGMAEUS

FLANGED FACES

Some male Bornean orangutans have flanges, or cheek pads, as well as throat sacs that are used to produce a call during mating. This is a sign of social hierarchy and dominance, as males will defend their territory from other males. Younger, subordinate males will develop flanges and throat sacs once their own territory is established.

GOLDEN SNUB-NOSED MONKEY *Rhinopithecus roxellana*

CONSERVATION STATUS: ENDANGERED

Golden snub-nosed monkeys live in Central and Southwest China in mountain forest habitats. Males grow long, golden hair on their neck while females have shorter hair and turn darker in color as they age. They are social animals and live in family groups consisting of one male, multiple females, and their offspring. Sometimes a herd of bachelor males live together. During summer months, many groups will come together, forming large bands in a behavior known as fission and fusion. They are mostly an arboreal species, spending most of their time in tree canopies; therefore, their diet is primarily food they can access from trees, such as leaves, fir or pine needles, buds, bark, fruit seeds, and lichen.

BY THE NUMBERS		CLASSIFICATION
5,200–13,000 FEET	Habitat elevation	KINGDOM: ANIMALIA
		PHYLUM: CHORDATA
		CLASS: MAMMALIA
		ORDER: PRIMATES
20–70	Group size during winter	SUBORDER: HAPLORHINI
		INFRAORDER: SIMIIFORMES
		FAMILY: CERCOPITHECIDAE
200	Group size during summer	GENUS: RHINOPITHECUS
		SPECIES: R. ROXELLANA

167

RHESUS MACAQUE *Macaca mulatta*

CONSERVATION STATUS: LEAST CONCERN

Rhesus macaques are native to South and Southeast Asia and can be found in a wide variety of habitats including forests, open scrub, high mountain regions, deserts, and even urban areas near humans. Rhesus macaques live in groups with multiple males, multiple females, and their offspring. Within each group, there is a hierarchy in both sexes. Males and females that are of equal ranking in hierarchy will mate.

BY THE NUMBERS	
14.1–17.6 OUNCES	Birth weight
8.1–9 INCHES	Tail length
30 YEARS	Lifespan

CLASSIFICATION

- **KINGDOM:** Animalia
- **PHYLUM:** Chordata
- **CLASS:** Mammalia
- **ORDER:** Primates
- **SUBORDER:** Haplorhini
- **INFRAORDER:** Simiiformes
- **FAMILY:** Cercopithecidae
- **GENUS:** Macaca
- **SPECIES:** M. mulatta

RAMPANT RHESUS

Rhesus macaques are very active and lively animals. They can often be seen running on all fours, jumping, climbing, swimming, or making a variety of facial expressions and audible sounds.

YELLOW BABOON *Papio cynocephalus*

CONSERVATION STATUS: LEAST CONCERN

Yellow baboons live in Eastern Africa in savannas, tropical rainforests, and grassland steppes. They are known for their yellowish-brown coat, purplish-black colored face, doglike muzzle, and hairless rump. In addition, males are also much larger in size than females, which helps to identify between sexes. Yellow baboons live in large social groups and communicate with each other through sounds and gestures. They are terrestrial animals that spend most of their time on the ground but sleep in the trees at night. Their diet consists of fruit, pods, grass, seeds, roots, flowers, leaves, insects, and occasionally meat.

BY THE NUMBERS	
50.7 POUNDS	*Average male weight*
26.5 POUNDS	*Average female weight*
20–180	*Group size*

CLASSIFICATION

- **KINGDOM:** ANIMALIA
- **PHYLUM:** CHORDATA
- **CLASS:** MAMMALIA
- **ORDER:** PRIMATES
- **SUBORDER:** HAPLORHINI
- **INFRAORDER:** SIMIIFORMES
- **FAMILY:** CERCOPITHECIDAE
- **GENUS:** PAPIO
- **SPECIES:** P. CYNOCEPHALUS

MONOTREMATA

Platypuses and Echidnas

The biological Monotremata order is made of platypuses and echidnas. Animals in this order lay eggs instead of having a live birth. They also have highly adapted snouts with no teeth.

ESTIMATED NUMBER OF MONOTREMATA SPECIES	5
DID YOU KNOW?	*Despite laying eggs, mother monotremes still nurse their young with milk.*

PLATYPUS
Ornithorhynchus anatinus

CONSERVATION STATUS: NEAR THREATENED

Platypuses live in Australia and Tasmania in rivers, lagoons, and streams and are classified as a semi-aquatic species. They are nocturnal, solitary animals that spend most of their time foraging for food. When they are not foraging, they can be found in their burrow, which is located along the water banks and contains many tunnels. Males also have sharp spurs on their back ankles that contain venom to ward off predators. A female platypus lays eggs in her burrow, where they will later hatch and she will nurse them until they can swim and forage on their own.

BY THE NUMBERS		CLASSIFICATION	
10–12 HOURS	*Daily time spent foraging*	KINGDOM:	ANIMALIA
		PHYLUM:	CHORDATA
10 DAYS	*For eggs to hatch*	CLASS:	MAMMALIA
		ORDER:	MONOTREMATA
4 MONTHS	*Duration that puggles (babies) nurse*	FAMILY:	ORNITHORHYNCHIDAE
		GENUS:	ORNITHORHYNCHUS
		SPECIES:	O. ANATINUS

PLATYPUS SWIMMING

Platypuses use their webbed feet to move through the water and their beaver-like tail to steer.

MONOTREMATA
Platypuses & Echidnas

ORNITHORHYNCHIDAE
Platypuses

DUGONGIDAE

TACHYGLOSSUS
Short-Beaked Echidnas

ZAGLOSSUS
Long-Beaked Echidnas

SHORT-BEAKED ECHIDNA *Tachyglossus aculeatus*

CONSERVATION STATUS: LEAST CONCERN

Short-beaked echidnas live in Australia, Tasmania, New Guinea, and Kangaroo Island. They can live in a variety of extreme habitats by burrowing in the soil or seeking shelter in hollowed out vegetation. They are nicknamed "spiny anteaters" because they use their long snouts and sharp claws to break through termite and ant nests and logs. They catch their prey by flicking their long, sticky tongue in and out of their mouth while swallowing insects.

BY THE NUMBERS		CLASSIFICATION
6.7 INCHES	Length of tongue	**KINGDOM:** Animalia **PHYLUM:** Chordata **CLASS:** Mammalia
4.41– 15.42 POUNDS	Body weight range	**ORDER:** Monotremata **FAMILY:** Tachyglossidae **GENUS:** Tachyglossus **SPECIES:** T. aculeatus
150– 200 DAYS	Duration puggles (babies) nurse	

PUGGLE POUCH

Female short-beaked echidnas lay one egg at a time. When puggles (babies) hatch, they are blind and hairless. Puggles then enter the mother's pouch, where they will nurse, grow, and continue to develop until their spines become too prickly, after which mothers will remove them and allow them to continue to nurse.

CAMELIDAE

Camels

The Camelidae family is made up of six species. Members of this family are large, have thin necks, long legs, and are herbivores.

ESTIMATED NUMBER OF CAMELIDAE SPECIES: 6

DID YOU KNOW? *Despite appearances, camelids lack hooves. Instead they have a thick, leathery footpad to walk on.*

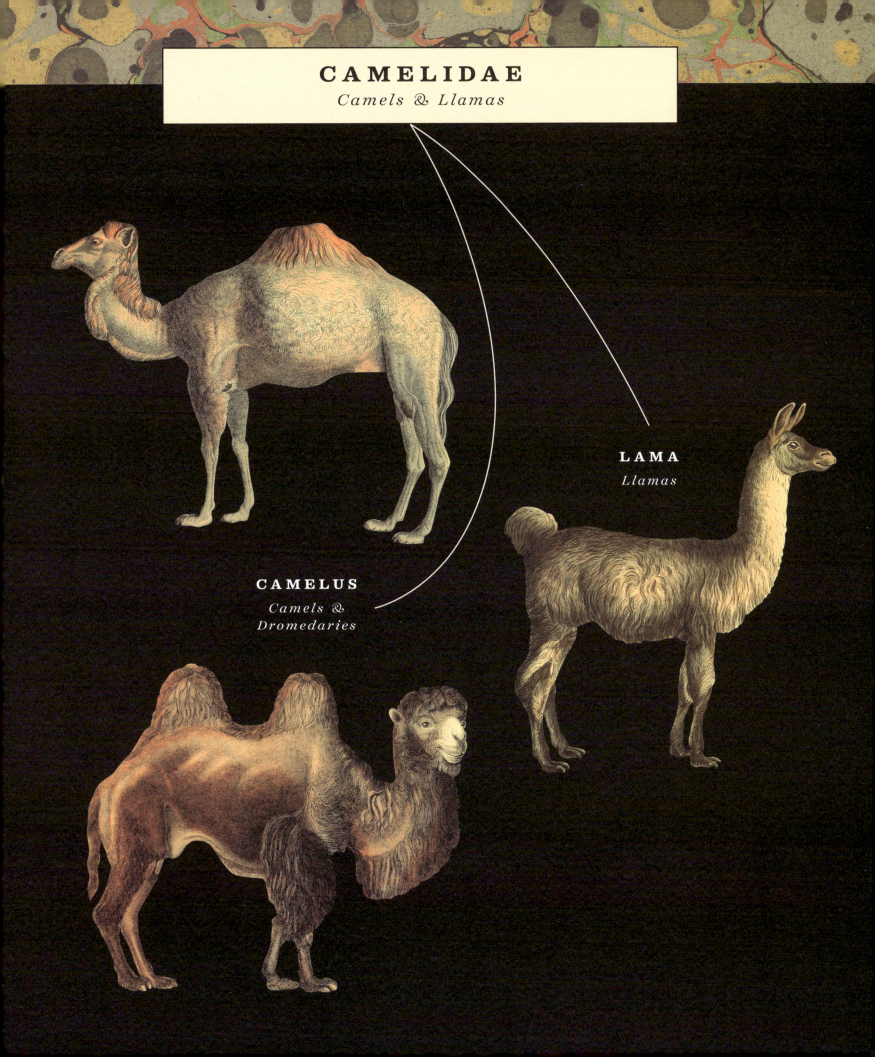

BACTRIAN CAMEL *Camelus bactrianus*

CONSERVATION STATUS: CRITICALLY ENDANGERED

Bactrian camels live in Central Asia in varying habitats, including the rocky desert mountains, sand dunes, and desert stony plains. They are easily identifiable by their two humps, which contain fatty tissue that is later converted into energy when needed. The health of the bactrian camel is apparent by looking at its humps: if they are upright, plump, and firm, the camel is healthy; however, sagging or humps leaning sideways is an indication that the camel is malnourished. Their thick insulating coat provides warmth during the winter; however, it is shed each summer, which helps to regulate their body temperature.

BY THE NUMBERS	
35 GALLONS	Water intake with one gulp
1,300–2,200 POUNDS	Weight range
30–35 YEARS	Lifespan

CLASSIFICATION

- **KINGDOM:** Animalia
- **PHYLUM:** Chordata
- **CLASS:** Mammalia
- **ORDER:** Artiodactyla
- **FAMILY:** Camelidae
- **GENUS:** Camelus
- **SPECIES:** C. bactrianus

DUST COVERS

Bactrian camels also have double layered eyelashes to prevent sand and dust from entering their eyes, and their nostrils can close to prevent sand from entering as well.

DROMEDARY *Camelus dromedarius*

CONSERVATION STATUS: NOT EVALUATED

Dromedaries, also called Arabian camels, live in areas of the Middle East, northern India, the Sahara desert of Africa, and portions of central Australia. They prefer habitats that have desert conditions with little rain. Dromedaries are a semi-domestic animal mostly used for riding, with the exception of the feral (wild) herds in Australia. Dromedaries spend nearly half of their day grazing and ruminating, as they primarily eat dry grasses, thorny plants, and saltbush. They typically live in small family groups, where they can be seen walking in a single file line with the female leading and the dominant male herding the group from behind.

BY THE NUMBERS	
5.5–6.5 FEETS	Height
6 MONTHS	Maximum time without food and water
4,000 YEARS AGO	Estimated first domestication

CLASSIFICATION

KINGDOM: ANIMALIA
PHYLUM: CHORDATA
CLASS: MAMMALIA
ORDER: ARTIODACTYLA
FAMILY: CAMELIDAE
GENUS: CAMELUS
SPECIES: C. DROMEDARIUS

ABOUT THE AUTHOR

Lindy Mattice has always had a deep love for animals. When she was just seven years old, her family joined a wildlife rehabilitation organization where Lindy spent countless hours caring for young, orphaned animals who were eventually released back into the wild. She also worked with a local group as a pet detective, helping train dogs to search for lost pets. She was a member of the FFA (Future Farmers of America) organization, where she competed on the horse judging team and showed sheep. Lindy received her bachelor of science degree in agriculture science from Cal Poly. She currently resides in Bakersfield, California, with her husband and three children. She loves their family's two dogs and cat and her weekly horseback riding lessons.

BUSHEL
& PECK
BOOKS

ABOUT BUSHEL & PECK BOOKS

Bushel & Peck Books is a children's publishing house with a special mission. Through our Book-for-Book Promise™, we donate one book to kids in need for every book we sell. Our beautiful books are given to kids through schools, libraries, local neighborhoods, shelters, nonprofits, and also to many selfless organizations who are working hard to make a difference. So thank you for purchasing this book! Because of you, another book will find its way into the hands of a child who needs it most.

OUR GIVING

We can't solve every problem in the world, but we believe children's books can help. Illiteracy is linked to many of the world's greatest challenges, including crime, school dropout rates, and drug use. Yet impressively, just the presence of books in a home can be a leg up for struggling kids. Unfortunately, many children in need find themselves without adequate access to age-appropriate books. One study found that low-income neighborhoods have, in some US cities, only one book for every three hundred kids (compared to thirteen books for every one child in middle-income neighborhoods). With our Book-for-Book Promise™, Bushel & Peck Books is putting quality children's books into the hands of as many kids as possible. We hope these books bring an increased interest in reading and learning, and with that, a greater chance for future success. To learn more about how we give, including our annual Giving Plan and commitment to carbon-neutral shipments, or to nominate a school or organization to receive free books, please visit bushelandpeckbooks.com.